TANDEM

The House of the Hatchet

A feast of horror ...

... His blurred outline reminded me of a crouching beast ... his face ... was a waxen mask of death ... from which two eyes glared ...

A mad beast is loose ... an ageless, eternal beast ...

... It grew and grew ... It spread its wings and sank into the sand ... nothing remained above the earth except a living head that twisted and struggled ... the Thing had wound its black paws around his neck and bitten him to death ...

... if your nerves can stand it.

The House of the Hatchet
and other tales of horror

Robert Bloch

TANDEM
14 Gloucester Road, London SW7

Originally published in the U.S.A. by Belmont
Productions Ltd.

Published in Great Britain by Tandem Books Limited,
1965
Reprinted by Universal-Tandem Publishing Co. Ltd,
1971

Made and printed in Great Britain by
C. Nicholls & Company Ltd.

CONTENTS

By Way of Introduction

"Where do you get the ideas for your stories?"

This is the question that haunts every writer.

The average author can provide a graceful and plausible answer. He is an "observer of life," or a "student of human nature." He is "interested in historical research" or he "draws on experience."

But what can the creator of fantasy reply?

He does not deal with life, but with matters beyond life. He cannot submit that he is a student of human nature – although *inhuman* nature is often a subject of his consideration. His historical research is confined to legend and mythology.

The usual preface to a collection of fantastic fiction consists of a dissertation on imaginative literature in general, and any consideration of the motives impelling the author in the creation of his own work is politely ignored.

No, the fantasy writer is hard put to answer this inevitable query regarding his source of inspiration. So hard put, in fact, that I have never read any attempt at explanation.

I can try to explain by reminding the reader that a fantasy author is definitely cast in the dual role of Jekyll and Hyde.

Dr. Jekyll (the writer in everyday life) is usually a normal enough individual. His wife does not fear him, his children will not scream when he appears, and friends or business associates seldom tremble in his presence.

But when kindly Dr. Jekyll retires to the privacy of his rooms and crouches over a low table, he is transformed

– by the simple alchemy of typewriter and paper – into the monstrous Hyde.

As in Stevenson's tale, the mask of humanity is ripped away; its very aspect forgotten by the being beneath. This creature, locked in a lonely room, knows nothing of the everyday world beyond. He has knowledge only of the worlds that *were* . . . that *will be* . . . and that *co-exist*.

A fearful wisdom, his. He knows what winds the witches ride, what spells the wizards weave. He has trafficked with the tenants of the tomb, and his body has lain in grave-earth beside the dreaded Vampire. For him there are no secrets in a madman's skull. His are eyes that gaze unflinchingly on the dread glory of the Medusa. His ears echo to the rustlings of maggots of the feast; his nostrils are suffused with odors of the Pit; his mouth is shapen for the fulfillment of strange hungers.

For, essentially, he is engaged upon the composition of a travelogue . . . the history of a voyage in the realms of pure imagination . . . a journey through a skull. And each tale is but a chapter in the endless odyssey.

Does this sound naïve, overly melodramatic?

If so, it is because frankness has long ceased to play a part in the personal depositions of author to reader. The author of fantasy, in particular, does his best to entirely conceal the emotional basis of his creative impulse.

Dr. Jekyll attempts to deny the very existence of Mr. Hyde.

But . . . Mr. Hyde exists.

My life as Jekyll has been commonplace in the extreme. I have a home, a family, a regular occupation, friends; a normal schedule of hobbies and amusements. Despite the betraying evidence of a somewhat flamboyant sense of humour, I am sure those who know Dr. Jekyll regard him as a rather prosy fellow.

Yet Mr. Hyde is active, nonetheless. It is a partnership which has proved both pleasant and profitable – and it would be ingratitude indeed if I allowed Dr. Jekyll to take the credit without proper acknowledgement to his *alter ego*.

In most of the stories assembled here, Jekyll is the conscious narrator. His style is often pseudo-scholarly, his imagery lurid and contrived. He is a conscious polysyllabophile, and his narrative technique owes much to the influence and guidance of the late H. P. Lovecraft.

But the inspiration comes from Mr. Hyde. He is definitely responsible for the basic theme underlying the stories as a whole ... the logical insistence that unpleasant consequences await anyone who meddles in matters best left undisturbed.

I fear, however, that Hyde must also share the blame for errors of taste and judgement. In his haste to effect some particularly ghastly revelation, he has ignored many literary niceties. I can only submit that this is a matter beyond my control. If, some time, I can write a tale dictated entirely by the conscious personality of Dr. Jekyll, the result may be entirely different from any effort presented here. But, barring this possibility, the works published under my name will continue to exhibit the hideous handiwork of Hyde.

And when anyone inquires as to where I get the ideas for my stories, I can only shrug and answer, "From my collaborator – Mr. Hyde."

– ROBERT BLOCH

Sweets to the Sweet

IRMA didn't look like a witch.

She had small, regular features, a peaches-and-cream complexion, blue eyes, and fair, almost ash-blonde hair. Besides she was only eight years old.

"Why does he tease her so?" sobbed Miss Pall. "That's where she got the idea in the first place – because he calls her a little witch."

Sam Steever bulked his paunch back into the squeaky swivel chair and folded his heavy hands in his lap. His fat lawyer's mask was immobile, but he was really quite distressed.

Women like Miss Pall should never sob. Their glasses wiggle, their thin noses twitch, their creasy eyelids redden, and their stringy hair becomes disarrayed.

"Please, control yourself," coaxed Sam Steever. "Perhaps if we could just talk this whole thing over sensibly –"

"I don't care!" Miss Pall sniffled. "I'm not going back there again. I can't stand it. There's nothing I can do, anyway. The man is your brother and she's your brother's child. It's not my responsibility. I've tried –"

"Of course you've tried." Sam Steever smiled benignly, as if Miss Pall were foreman of a jury. "I quite understand. But I still don't see why you are so upset, dear lady."

Miss Pall removed her spectacles and dabbed at her eyes with a floral-print handkerchief. Then she deposited the soggy ball in her purse, snapped the catch, replaced her spectacles, and sat up straight.

"Very well, Mr. Steever," she said. "I shall do my best to acquaint you with my reasons for quitting your brother's employ."

She suppressed a tardy sniff.

"I came to John Steever two years ago in response to an advertisement for a housekeeper, as you know. When I found that I was to be governess to a motherless six year old child, I was at first distressed. I know nothing of the care of children."

"John had a nurse the first six years," Sam Steever nodded. "You know Irma's mother died in childbirth."

"I am aware of that," said Miss Pall, primly. "Naturally, one's heart goes out to a lonely, neglected little girl. And she was so terribly lonely, Mr Steever – if you could have seen her, moping around in the corners of the big, ugly old house."

"I have seen her," said Sam Steever hastily, hoping to forestall another outburst. "And I know what you've done for Irma. My brother is inclined to be thoughtless, even a bit selfish at times. He doesn't understand."

"He's cruel," declared Miss Pall, suddenly vehement. "Cruel and wicked. Even if he is your brother, I say he's no fit father for any child. When I came there, her little arms were black and blue from beatings. He used to take a belt –"

"I know. Sometimes, I think John never recovered from the shock of Mrs Steever's death. That's why I was so pleased when you came, dear lady. I thought you might help the situation."

"I tried," Miss Pall whimpered. "You know I tried. I never raised a hand to that child in two years, though many's the time your brother has told me to punish her. 'Give the little witch a beating' he used to say. 'That's all she needs – a good thrashing.' And then she'd hide behind my back and whisper to me to protect her. But she

12

wouldn't cry, Mr Steever. Do you know, I've never seen her cry."

Sam Steever felt vaguely irritated and a bit bored. He wished the old hen would get on with it. So he smiled and oozed treacle. "But just what is your problem, dear lady?"

"Everything was all right when I came there. We got along just splendidly. I started to teach Irma to read – and was surprised to find that she had already mastered reading. Your brother disclaimed having taught her, but she spent hours curled up on the sofa with a book. 'Just like her,' he used to say. 'Unnatural little witch. Doesn't play with the other children. Little witch.' That's the way he kept talking, Mr Steever. As if she were some sort of – I don't know what. And she so sweet and quiet and pretty!

"Is it any wonder she read? I used to be that way myself when I was a girl, because – but never mind.

"Still, it was a shock that day I found her looking through the Encyclopedia Britannica. 'What are you reading, Irma?' I asked. She showed me. It was the article on Witchcraft.

"You see what morbid thoughts your brother has inculcated in her poor little head?

"I did my best. I went out and bought her some toys – she had absolutely nothing, you know; not even a doll. She didn't even know how to *play*! I tried to get her interested in some of the other little girls in the neighborhood, but it was no use. They didn't understand her and she didn't understand them. There were scenes. Children can be cruel, thoughtless. And her father wouldn't let her go to public school. I was to teach her –

"Then I brought her the modelling clay. She liked that. She would spend hours just making faces with clay. For a child of six Irma displayed real talent.

"We made little dolls together, and I sewed clothes for them. That first year was a happy one, Mr Steever. Particularly during those months when your brother was away in South America. But this year, when he came back – oh, I can't bear to talk about it!"

"Please," said Sam Steever. "You must understand. John is not a happy man. The loss of his wife, the decline of his import trade, and his drinking – but you know all that."

"All I know is that he hates Irma," snapped Miss Pall, suddenly. "He hates her. He wants her to be bad, so he can whip her. 'If you don't discipline the little witch, I shall,' he always says. And then he takes her upstairs and thrashes her with his belt – you must do something, Mr. Steever, or I'll go to the authorities myself."

The crazy old biddy would at that, Sam Steever thought. Remedy – more treacle. "But about Irma," he persisted.

"She's changed, too. Ever since her father returned this year. She won't play with me any more, hardly looks at me. It is, as though I failed her, Mr. Steever, in not protecting her from that man. Besides – she thinks she's a witch."

Crazy. Stark, staring crazy. Sam Steever creaked upright in his chair.

"Oh you needn't look at me like that, Mr. Steever. She'll tell you so herself – if you ever visited the house!"

He caught the reproach in her voice and assuaged it with a deprecating nod.

"She told me all right, if her father wants her to be a witch she'll be a witch. And she won't play with me, or anyone else, because witches don't play. Last Halloween she wanted me to give her a broomstick. Oh, it would be funny if it weren't so tragic. That child is losing her sanity.

14

"Just a few weeks ago I thought she'd changed. That's when she asked me to take her to church one Sunday. 'I want to see the baptism,' she said. Imagine that – an eight-year-old interested in baptism! Reading too much, that's what does it.

"Well, we went to church and she was as sweet as can be, wearing her new blue dress and holding my hand. I was proud of her, Mr. Steever, really proud.

"But after that, she went right back into her shell. Reading around the house, running through the yard at twilight and talking to herself.

"Perhaps it's because your brother wouldn't bring her a kitten. She was pestering him for a black cat, and he asked why, and she said, 'Because witches always have black cats.' Then he took her upstairs.

"I can't stop him, you know. He beat her again the night the power failed and we couldn't find the candles. He said she'd stolen them. Imagine that – accusing an eight-year-old child of stealing candles!

"That was the beginning of the end. Then today, when he found his hairbrush missing –"

"You say he beat her with his hairbrush?"

"Yes. She admitted having stolen it. Said she wanted it for her doll."

"But didn't you say she has no dolls?"

"She made one. At least I think she did. I've never seen it – she won't show us anything any more; won't talk to us at table, just impossible to handle her.

"But this doll she made – it's a small one, I know, because at times she carries it tucked under her arm. She talks to it and pets it, but she won't show it to me or to him. He asked her about the hairbrush and she said she took it for the doll.

"Your brother flew into a terrible rage – he'd been drinking in his room again all morning, oh don't think I don't know it! – and she just smiled and said he could have it now. She went over to her bureau and handed it to him. She hadn't harmed it in the least; his hair was still in it, I noticed.

"But he snatched it up, and then he started to strike her about the shoulders with it, and he twisted her arm and then he –"

Miss Pall huddled in her chair and summoned great racking sobs from her thin chest.

Sam Steever patted her shoulder, fussing about her like an elephant over a wounded canary.

"That's all, Mr Steever. I came right to you. I'm not even going back to that house to get my things. I can't stand any more – the way he beat her – and the way she didn't cry, just giggled and giggled and giggled – sometimes I think she *is* a witch – that he made her into a witch –"

Sam Steever picked up the phone. The ringing had broken the relief of silence after Miss Pall's hasty departure.

"Hello – that you, Sam?"

He recognised his brother's voice, somewhat the worse for drink.

"Yes, John."

"I suppose the old bat came running straight to you to shoot her mouth off."

"If you mean Miss Pall, I've seen her, yes."

"Pay no attention. I can explain everything."

"Do you want me to stop in? I haven't paid you a visit in months."

"Well – not right now. Got an appointment with the doctor this evening."

"Something wrong?"

"Pain in my arm. Rheumatism or something. Getting

a little diathermy. But I'll call you tomorrow and we'll straighten this whole mess out."

"Right."

But John Steever did not call the next day. Along about supper time, Sam called him.

Surprisingly enough, Irma answered the phone. Her thin, squeaky little voice sounded faintly in Sam's ears.

"Daddy's upstairs sleeping. He's been sick."

"Well don't disturb him. What is it, his arm?"

"His back, now. He has to go to the doctor again in a little while."

"Tell him I'll call tomorrow, then. Uh – everything all right, Irma? I mean, don't you miss Miss Pall?"

"No. I'm glad she went away. She's stupid."

"Oh. Yes. I see. But you phone me if you want anything. And I hope your Daddy's better."

"Yes. So do I," said Irma, and then she began to giggle, and then she hung up.

There was no giggling the following afternoon when John Steever called Sam at the office. His voice was sober – with the sharp sobriety of pain.

"Sam – for God's sake, get over here. Something's happening to me!"

"What's the trouble?"

"The pain – it's killing me! I've got to see you, quickly."

"There's a client in the office, but I'll get rid of him. Say, wait a minute. Why don't you call the doctor?"

"That quack can't help me. He gave me diathermy for my arm and yesterday he did the same thing for my back."

"Didn't it help."

"The pain went away, yes. But it's back now. I feel – like I was being crushed. Squeezed, here in the chest. I can't breathe."

"Sounds like pleurisy. Why don't you call him?"

"It isn't pleurisy. He examined me. Said I was sound as a dollar. No, there's nothing organically wrong. And I couldn't tell him the real cause."

"Real cause?"

"Yes. The pins. The pin that little fiend is sticking into the doll she made. Into the arm, the back. And now heaven only knows how she's causing *this.*"

"John, you mustn't –"

"Oh what's the use of talking? I can't move off the bed here. She has me now. I can't go down and stop her, get hold of the doll. And nobody else would believe it. But it's the doll all right, the one she made with the candle-wax and the hair from my brush. Oh – it hurts to talk – that cursed little witch! Hurry, Sam. Promise you'll do something – anything – get that doll from her – get that doll –"

Half an hour later, at four-thirty, Sam Steever entered his brother's house.

Irma opened the door.

It gave Sam a shock to see her standing there, smiling and unperturbed, pale blonde hair brushed immaculately back from the rosy oval of her face. She looked just like a little doll. A little doll –

"Hello, Uncle Sam."

"Hello, Irma. Your Daddy called me, did he tell you? He said he wasn't feeling well –"

"I know. But he's all right now. He's sleeping."

Something happened to Sam Steever; a drop of ice-water trickled down his spine.

"Sleeping?" he croaked. "Upstairs?"

Before she opened her mouth to answer he was bounding up the steps to the second floor, striding down the hall to John's bedroom.

18

John lay on the bed. He was asleep, and only asleep. Sam Steever noted the regular rise and fall of his chest as he breathed. His face was calm, relaxed.

Then the drop of ice-water evaporated, and Sam could afford to smile and murmur "nonsense" under his breath as he turned away.

As he went downstairs he hastily improvised plans. A six-month vacation for his brother; avoid calling it a "cure." An orphanage for Irma; give her a chance to get away from this morbid old house, all these books . . .

He paused halfway down the stairs. Peering over the banister through the twilight he saw Irma on the sofa, cuddled up like a little white ball. She was talking to something she cradled in her arms, rocking it to and fro.

Then there was a doll, after all.

Sam Steever tip-toed very quietly down the stairs and walked over to Irma.

"Hello," he said.

She jumped. Both arms rose to cover completely whatever it was she had been fondling. She squeezed it tightly.

Sam Steever thought of a doll being squeezed across the chest –

Irma stared up at him, her face a mask of innocence. In the half-light her face did resemble a mask. The mask of a little girl, covering – what?

"Daddy's better now, isn't he?" lisped Irma.

"Yes, much better."

"I knew he would be."

"But I'm afraid he's going to have to go away for a rest. A long rest."

A smile filtered through the mask. "Good," said Irma.

"Of course," Sam went on, "you couldn't stay here all alone. I was wondering – maybe we could send you off to school, or to some kind of a home –"

19

Irma giggled. ''Oh, you needn't worry about me,'' she said. She shifted about on the sofa as Sam sat down, then sprang up quickly as he came close to her.

Her arms shifted with the movement, and Sam Steever saw a pair of tiny legs dangling down below her elbow. There were trousers on the legs, and little bits of leather for shoes.

"What's that you have, Irma?" he asked. "Is it a doll?" Slowly, he extended his pudgy hand.

She pulled back.

"You can't see it," she said.

"But I want to. Miss Pall said you made such lovely ones."

"Miss Pall is stupid. So are you. Go away."

"Please, Irma. Let me see it."

But even as he spoke, Sam Steever was staring at the top of the doll, momentarily revealed when she backed away. It was a head all right, with wisps of hair over a white face. Dusk dimmed the features, but Sam recognised the eyes, the nose, the chin –

He could keep up the pretence no longer.

"Give me that doll, Irma!" he snapped. "I know what it is. I know *who* it is –"

For an instant, the mask slipped from Irma's face, and Sam Steever stared into naked fear.

She knew, she knew he knew.

Then, just as quickly, the mask was replaced.

Irma was only a sweet, spoiled, stubborn little girl as she shook her head merrily and smiled with impish mischief in her eyes.

"Oh Uncle Sam," she giggled. "You're so silly! Why, this isn't a *real* doll."

"What is it, then?" he muttered.

Irma giggled once more, raising the figure as she spoke. "Why, it's only – candy!" Irma said.

20

"Candy?"

Irma nodded. Then, very swiftly, she slipped the tiny head of the image into her mouth.

And bit it off.

There was a single piercing scream from upstairs.

As Sam Steever turned and ran up the stairs, little Irma, still gravely munching, skipped out of the front door and into the night beyond.

The Dream-Makers

I'VE got the right lead for it. That's easy. I can start out with all the usual blah – Hollywood is a crazy town, filled with crazy people, and the craziest things happen there. I can give this yarn the old build-up.

But there's only one trouble. It *isn't* a yarn, and it happened to *me*.

So let's just take it from the top, with me climbing into my car that afternoon and heading out Wiltshire towards a place called Restlawn. It was just another assignment, and if *Filmdom* magazine wanted to do a series on *Grand Old-Timers of the Movies*, I was their man. Their hungry man.

I headed out past the Miracle Mile and into Beverly Hills taking it slow and avoiding the Freeway. I didn't particularly care for this job.

Grand Old-Timers. That's what cooled me. I knew what I was getting into – nosing around the Actor's Home and Central Casting, following leads that ended up in cheap flophouses and the gutters of Main Street.

That's where the *Grand Old-Timers* were, most of them. The men and women who "grew up with the Industry" until the Industry out-grew them. Oh, Pickford, Cooper, Gable and a few others didn't have to worry. They'd survived or retired gracefully on their savings. Valentino and Chaney and Fairbanks don't have to worry, either, because they died at the height of their success.

But what about the ones who weren't lucky enough to die while they were famous – Griffith, and Langdon, and Barrymore, struggling along until the all-too-bitter end?

And what about those who hadn't died yet – Sennett and Lloyd and Gish, and a dozen others? They'd be considered *Grand Old-Timers*, too.

I sighed, turning off Wiltshire past Westwood Village and seeking the smaller side-streets. I knew all about the *Grand Old-Timers*. The "special awards" trotted out for them at Academy banquets, and the doors slammed in their faces the next day. The humiliating "bit roles" played in occasional way-back-when films; the over publicized "come-backs" that puffed them up for one picture, then deflated them again to extra status.

It would be painful for them to be interviewed by me – and equally painful for me to do the job.

But a man must eat. And a man must dream . . .

They'd never be *Grand Old-Timers* to me, because of the dreams; the dreams they'd manufactured for my consumption thirty years ago. My dreams are still very much alive, and so are their creators.

Right now, riding down into Santa Monica, I found myself back in one of the great dreams – the great nightmare.

It's a warm fall Wednesday night in Maywood, Illinois. The year is 1925, and tonight is its climatic moment. Because you're eight years old, and you're going to the Lido, all by yourself at night, just like a grown-up. Sure, there's school tomorrow but gee Ma, just this once, you promised, I won't be home too late, and I want to see it so bad.

You have eight blocks to walk, eight exciting blocks through autumn darkness, with the dime for the show in the right hand and the nickel for the candy-bar in the left hand.

The Lido is a Palace. Its doors are guarded by marble columns a hundred feet high, but you don't just go right in. First you must look at all the pictures outside – the big ones in colour and the little ones that are like photographs.

There's this beautiful woman with the long hair and the man with the mask. And here the woman is standing on top of a tall building with another man in a soldier's uniform. He's got a moustache – he must be the hero.

But there's the man with the mask, spying on them. You can't see his face. He's up on some big statue and he looks mad, even with the mask on. That must be him, all right. That must be him.

But it's almost seven, the show is going to start, so you go up to that glittering cage and give your dime to the pretty girl with the lovely costume on. She smiles, and punches some machine, and out comes your ticket. Then you walk in and give your ticket to the man at the door. He smiles, too. You've already bought your candy-bar at the store next to the show, and you're all set.

It's wonderful in the Lido, even the lobby is wonderful. All red carpets and fancy chairs and a big bubbler with the water running all the time – not like at home where you got to turn the water off on account of the water bill being so high.

And it's even better inside, in the dark. Because there must be a thousand seats to choose from, all plush and soft, and when you sit down right spang in the centre of the show and count the rows ahead and the rows behind and look to see if any of the kids from school are there to see you sitting all alone like a grown-up, why then you just naturally look up at the sky.

Sure, they've got a sky at the Lido, just as blue as outside at night, and – it has stars in it! Honest, it has regular stars that twinkle! And all along the walls are statues, lighted up kind of dim, and the stars are shining, and it's more beautiful than any real palace you've ever seen.

Then the light goes on up at the left side of the stage and it's the organ. A real pretty lady plays the organ;

she has gold hair that kind of sparkles when the light hits it. But you don't look, now – you listen.

You sort of skooch down in your seat, all soft and snug, and look at the blue sky and the stars, and let the music just ooze over you. That organ must be just about the most wonderful kind of thing to play, and it plays everything, *Valencia* and *Blue Skies* and that song, *Collegiate*, that they played when Harold Lloyd was in *The Freshman*.

But now the light is going out, except for the little one right over the keys, and the music is changing to a sort of loud exciting noise, and the curtain is going back, just like magic, and the side-lights blink off, and there is the movie, all lighted up.

And first off it's *Topics of the Day*, which is just a lot of grown-up jokes one after the other, in writing on the screen. The organ makes fiddle-around noises but it isn't very interesting, not like the pictures. But then comes *Felix the Cat* and that little mouse is in it and the old farmer guy with the bald head and the beard. Funniest part is where Felix chases him through the haystack with the pitchfork and he falls in the well and comes up and spits out the water and a fish comes right out of his mouth.

But the real comedy is even better. It's got Billy Dooley in his sailor suit – Billy Dooley is one of the best ones, better than Bobby Vernon or Al St. John, but not quite as good as Lloyd Hamilton and Larry Semon or Lupino Lane. This one is real funny and everybody laughs. Billy Dooley, he jumps up in the air and sort of wig-wags his feet three times before coming down again. How do they do that?

Then the music pounds away and the comedy is over and they turn the lights blue for a minute. The big picture is coming – the one you've been waiting to see. You can tell by the lights and the kind of music that it's a real spooky picture. There's this man in the mask, and he wants to get the girl and he hangs this one guy in the cellar. Then he does get her, and takes her down to his secret hiding place where he sleeps in a coffin and plays the organ. He's sitting there playing with his mask on, and the girl sneaks up behind him, and you know what she's going to do now and you're waiting.

All at once she does it; she pulls off the mask. And the face comes up to fill the screen, rushes out of the screen and blots out everything until there's nothing else in the world but that grinning flesh-covered skull with the rotting fangs and the glaring eyes that you're going to dream about tonight and every night.

And that's the dream you got from Lon Chaney ...

Oh, they made real dreams in those days. There's never been a monster since to equal Chaney, never a villain as arrogant as Stroheim, never a heroine as lovely as Barbara La Marr or a hero as rugged and determined as William S. Hart.

All of it came back from a million years ago, and then it was gone and I was riding down Caprice Drive and the sun was shining.

The sun shone on the *Restlawn* sign. I parked, walked up the drive, poked the buzzer. Chimes sounded.

The woman who opened the door wore a starched uniform. Her hair was starched and her eyes were starched, too. Stiff, sanatorium-face, stiff sanatorium-voice.

"I beg your pardon. I'm from *Filmdom* magazine. To see Mr. Franklin."

"Have you an appointment?"

"I called this morning."

"Room 216. That's on the second floor, front."

I took the stairs. I walked slowly, not relishing this, dreading what I might expect to find. A whitehaired old man, sitting at the window of a private hospital room; sitting and staring out at the living in the streets and then staring back at the pictures of the dead lining his walls. *To Jeffrey Franklin, the world's greatest director.* Signed – Mickey Neilan, Mabel Normand, Lowell Sherman, John Gilbert.

Well, supposing they were dead, and supposing he was sick, and old? He was still the world's greatest director. For my money and a lot of other people's money. Hadn't made a picture since that last floppola in '29, when sound really came in. But before that, he'd been one of the true dream-makers.

Let's see, that was twenty-four, almost twenty-five years ago. Hard to imagine him still alive. Must be older than God. This was going to be sad, very sad. But a man must eat . . .

I knocked discreetly on the door of 216. The voice called, "Come in." I opened the door and entered.

And the new dream began . . .

2

IN the publicity shots I'd seen of him a quarter-century ago, Jeffrey Franklin had appeared as a tall, black-haired man, smoking a curved-stem pipe. He was always pictured standing, legs apart, feet firmly planted, chin jutting forth aggressively.

Seeing Jeffrey Franklin in the doorway now was quite a shock.

He was a tall, black-haired man, smoking a curved-stem pip. He stood with his legs apart, feet firmly planted, chin jutting forth aggressively.

I guess I stared.

"Come in and make yourself comfortable," he invited.

It wasn't difficult to make myself comfortable – because 216 turned out to be a suite. There were at least two other rooms leading off the big parlour, and the parlour itself was more than spacious.

No hospital bed, no tattered clippings or faded photos on the walls, no institutionally uncomfortable furniture; instead, I found myself in a modern masculine *decor* that deserved to be called luxurious. The whole atmosphere was very definitely present-time. And so was Jeffrey Franklin.

"Get you a drink?"

"Here?" My voice implied the sanatorium surroundings and he smiled.

"I'm a paying guest, not a patient. Little alchohol tones the system, I find. Keeps a man from getting old."

"It certainly seems to work." I blurted it out tactlessly, but he smiled again.

"Type-casting would put you down for scotch and water. Right?"

"Right."

"Speaking of type-casting, what do you think of Frisbie?"

"Who?"

"Miss Frisbie. The dragon who guards the portals. Isn't she perfect for the role?"

I nodded. Even before he placed the drink in my hand, I felt at ease.

I chose a lounge chair and Jeffrey Franklin made a gracefully self-conscious picture on the sofa across from me. He looked a bit like those man-of-distinction ads they used to run a few years back, and (as my thoughts grew still more remote) like one of the old-time Shakespearean hams. Come to think of it, hadn't he started out as a rep player in legit?

The question reminded me of my errand, and abruptly

I felt embarrassed once again. He sensed it immediately; his perception was remarkable for a man his age. (Good Lord, how old *was* he? He had to be close to seventy. The whole set-up mystified me.)

"It isn't easy, is it?" His voice, like his smile was soft.

"What isn't easy?"

"Being a ghoul." He raised his hand. "I don't mean it unkindly, son. I know you're just doing a job, getting your story. But I wish I had a nickel for every inquiring reporter who has come out here, spade in hand, to dig up the remains during the past twenty-odd years."

"You've been here that long?"

He nodded. "Right here. Ever since *Revolution*."

"Your last picture."

"My last picture. The flop." There was no discernible emotion in his voice.

"But why – ?"

"I like it here."

"But you're not sick, and if you'll permit me to say so, it doesn't look as if you're broke, either. And you could have had other pictures, there were contracts waiting for you, and –"

"I like it here."

He leaned forward. "I'm afraid I can't give you much of a sob-story. And neither can Walter Harland, or Peggy Dorr, or Danny Keene, or any of the other regulars in my old company. None of us was shoved out, none of us is on relief. You'll have a hard time forcing the tears for this scene."

It was my turn to lean forward. "Mr. Franklin, I'd like to set you straight on one thing. I'm not looking for a sob-story. I wouldn't write it if I found it. Believe me, nothing pleases me more than to know you're here by choice. I don't like anything to happen to my dreams."

"Your dreams?" He dropped the man-of-distinction

pose. The long hands joined across his knees, and I noted with vague satisfaction that the backs were free of the tell-tale mottled markings of age. "What do you mean by dreams?" he asked.

So I told him, or tried to tell him. About Chaney in *The Phantom of the Opera*. The dream about Keaton in *The Genaral*. Doug sliding down the drape in *Robin Hood*, Charlie eating the shoe. Renee Adoree stumbling after the truck in *The Big Parade*; half-a-hundred memorable moments that somehow stick in my mind with a greater sense of reality than the contemporary events of the childhood I lived through during the time I saw the pictures.

I guess I talked a long while. About the films, and the actors, and the directors of the silent days. About the effect of the organ music, the auto-hypnosis which was rudely shattered by the theatrical phoniness of sound. I wondered out loud whether or not I was alone in my experience or viewpoint; how many hundreds or thousands or millions of others (trending along towards middle age, now, and it's hard to realize that) who might share the illusions of the great days when the "silver screen" was really silver and shimmered with a strange enchantment.

And I tried to figure why it had changed. Was it that I was no longer a child, had grown up? No – because I've seen some of the films again, since then, at special showings; *Caligari*, of course, *Zorro*, *Intolerance*, a dozen others. And the last reels of *The Strong Man* are just as funny, the scene in *The Thief* where Doug conjures up the army from the dust is still pure enchantment.

Well – wondering out loud – was it radio, or television, or the smart-aleck "inside stuff" attitude adopted generally in a world where everybody was busy dispensing the "low-down" on celebrities?

Was it the war, the post-war era, the new age of fear;

had the Bomb done more than split the atom, had it also shattered the dreams?

"Such stuff as dreams are made of." Yes, Franklin was an old repertory ham, all right. He rolled out the quotation with sonorous relish, but I sensed the sincerity behind it.

"Odd that you've speculated along those lines," he mused. "I didn't think anyone else but ourselves had noticed the change." He noted my look. "Walter Harland and Tom Humphrey, some of the others, still get together and reminisce. You'll probably be talking to them, if you're planning a series of articles. They've aged pretty gracefully, you'll find."

I took the opening. "I hope you won't be offended if I report the same thing about you," I said. "Frankly, I can't get over seeing you like this. I admit I expected –"

"This?" Jeffrey Franklin rose and abruptly disappeared. In his place was a bent, hobbling oldster with withered, claw-like fingers scrabbling at a wobbly chin. Once again I remembered, too, that one of his tricks as a director was to play every role for the benefit of his actors before doing a take.

He straightened up, resumed his seat. "The years have been kind. Everything has gone well since *Revolution*. That was my only mistake, thinking I could go against their wishes. I haven't tried to change the plot since, and neither has Walter or Tom or Peggy, any of the others."

My ears stood up, my forepaw raised, and I came to the point. I smelled *story* here. "Plot?" I said. "Then there is something to all those rumours – they did try to force you out when sound came and the studio reorganized. I suppose they threatened the company with the blacklist and squeezed you out with a stock reshuffle?"

Jeffrey Franklin did a very odd thing. He looked up at

the ceiling and I could have sworn he was *listening* for a moment before he answered. Once a ham, always a ham.

But his answer, when he gave it was casual. "Sorry to disappoint you once again. I told you we weren't forced out, and that's the truth. Check with the others. They all had offers, plenty of offers. Most of them had legitimate stage experience, and they could have switched to the talkies without any trouble. But we decided it was time to quit while we were ahead of the game. As I say, *Revolution* flopped. And there were other examples; people who didn't have sense to quit when they should."

"You mean Gilbert, and Lew Cody and Charles Ray, people like that?"

"Perhaps. But I was thinking specifically of Roland Blade, Fay Terris, Matty Ryan."

Funny how the names took on long-forgotten meanings to me.

Roland Blade, whose name belonged up there with Navarro and LaRoque and Ricardo Cortez – yes, he'd done a talkie or two, and then he went over the cliff in his fancy car. Fay Terris was vintage stuff, a sort of American Negri. Come to think of it, she'd made a few sound films before the fire in her beach-house. Ryan I didn't recall very well. He'd been an independent producer and a rather big one; something like Thomas Ince. Let's see, whatever happened to him? Suddenly I remembered the headlines. He'd been one of the early aviation enthusiasts, like Mary Astor's first husband. He crashed, and they found his body cut almost in two –

Odd. Very odd. They all met violent deaths. And now I could recall a half-dozen more, all around that time. Some were mysterious suicides. One had been the victim of a still-unsolved murder. Others perished in freak fires, drowned, disappeared.

"Do you mean you were superstitious about going

along with the new era and making talking pictures?" I asked.

Franklin smiled. "Once a reporter, always a reporter," he said. "Putting words in peoples' mouths. Please don't quote me to that effect, because I don't mean any such thing at all." He paused, and once again his eyes sought the ceiling before he continued.

"If anything, I mean that we were all at the same point when the change came to Hollywood. We'd all started around the turn of the 'twenties, made our names together, did our best work and reaped the rewards at the same time. The best times were past, for most of the silent stars, directors, producers. All that remained was the struggle to stay on top, the resultant strain, the recklessness which would inevitably invade our personal life-patterns and which resulted in tragedy for those who chose to stay on. They used to call it 'going Hollywood.' You remember the stories of Lloyd Hamilton's fancy parties, and Tom Mix with his sixteen-thousand-dollar car, and the things that happened to people like poor Wally Reid, Arbuckle, and the rest of the crowd.

"No, we just decided to quit, and that's all. I'm afraid it's not a very sensational lead for you."

I made one last try. "Didn't you say something about 'going against their wishes' and something about a 'plot?' "

Jeffrey Franklin rose. "You misunderstood me," he said. "I was speaking of our wishes, as a group, to leave films. And I've already told you there was no plot. Now, if you'll excuse me – I'm rather tired. But I've enjoyed this interview very much."

He was lying, and I knew it.

But there was nothing else to do but shake hands and head for the door. I smiled at him. And he looked at the ceiling ...

3

I walked into the little bookstore still wondering if I had the right address. Nobody was out front, and only a single bulb burned over the table at the rear of the shop. A stocky, middle-aged, bespectacled man dropped his book on the table and looked up at me.

"Yes?"

"I'm looking for Walter Harland."

The man stood up. He was taller than I'd thought, and not nearly as old as he seemed at first glance. He took off his glasses and smiled. And there, of course, stood Walter Harland.

There was something quite dramatic in the very simplicity of the revelation. And something else, something vaguely frightening. He was too young. Franklin was too young. They looked the way they had back in '29 or '30.

I wrestled the thought, two falls out of three, while I introduced myself, explained my errand, and alluded to my visit with Jeffrey Franklin.

Walter Harland nodded. "I expected you," he said. "Mr. Franklin w– told me that you might visit me."

"It was kind of Mr. Franklin to w– tell you," I answered. He got it, and lowered his eyes.

"Don't say anything," I went on. "I can understand. This sort of thing isn't exactly my idea of good taste, either."

That got a smile out of him, and an invitation to sit down. I went through the same routine with him as I did with Franklin and got virtually the same answers. I began to wonder if Franklin hadn't given them all mimeographed copies of a script to memorize.

Yes, he had other offers when Franklin's production

unit disbanded. No, he hadn't wanted to continue. Yes, he had plenty of money to live on; he'd bought this bookstore and was quite content. He'd discovered it was much more pleasant to read other people's plots than to act them out.

I had to make the effort, then. "What's all this about plots?' I asked. "There's a rumour going round that you are the victim of some kind of plot to force you into obscurity."

It would be appropriately dramatic, at this moment, to report that Walter Harland gasped and turned pale. But actually he merely choked on his cigarette smoke – and if he had any dermatological reaction at all, the light was much too dim to disclose it.

"Don't believe everything you hear," he said, when his brief choking-spell was over with. "This isn't a B-movie, you know. I assure you, we got out because it was time. True, we talked it over, but we talked sensibly. And we agreed it was time to quit."

"Because you were all at the height of your fame, and you had reaped the rewards and didn't want to go downhill," I finished for him. "Is that it?"

"Precisely." He was happy now. We were back on the script again. I wished I could leave him there, but a man has to eat. So I gave him my sweetest smile and let him have it right between the eyes.

"I've heard that song before," I said, "and I don't buy it. Not a note rings true. Listen, Mr. Harland – I don't mean this to be offensive, but merely as a statement of known fact. Back in the twenties, you had a reputation for being one of the biggest hams in the business. Oh, I'm not casting any reflections on your ability as an actor. You were good, and everybody knows it. It's right down there in the book.

"But you were a ham, like all the rest. You always

35

played it big because you loved it that way. Signing autographs. Posing in those satin dressing-gowns, with the initials on the lapels, yet. Attending premiers in your Rolls, with the flappers kissing the tyres. Dragging those wolf-hounds into the Montmartre. That was your meat, wasn't it?"

He chuckled; a good, hearty actor's chuckle. "I suppose so. But a man gets older. He grows up."

"Listen, Peter Pan — actors never grow up in that sense of the word, and you know it! Nothing could make a matinee idol like you give up the glamour routine. Nothing except, perhaps, an awful scare of some kind. Come on now, what was it?"

I felt pretty proud of my D.A. routine, because it seemed to work. He sat there, breathing heavily for a long moment. Then he spoke.

"All right," he said softly. "There was a scare. An awful scare. Remember the films I played in? The fencing sequences, the fights, the acrobatics — Fairbanks stuff? That's what I was identified with. One day I went to the doctor for a routine checkup. He got excited, took cardiograms. You know the answer. My ticker was going bad. He warned me to take things easy if I wanted to be around for encores."

For a moment I was a little ashamed of myself. Then that word "warned" cropped up again. And I remembered that if I could play the D.A., Walter Harland could play the part of a man with a bad heart. And I realized that before he'd spoken, he'd looked up at the ceiling.

Maybe there was a fly up there, buzzing around. But something else kept buzzing in my brain.

I didn't say a word. I just shook my head.

He was already on his feet, ready to finish the script that Jeffrey Franklin had so carefully prepared. He held out his hand, then hesitated.

"You really want to know, don't you?" he said softly. "Not just to get an article, but because it means something to you."

I nodded.

"I'm afraid there's no way of explaining." He led me to the door, paused, put his hand on my shoulder. "Do you enjoy reading?" he asked.

"Yes."

"So do I. I've had a lot of time for it these past twenty years and more. I was particularly impressed with the writings of a man named Charles Fort. You know his work? Good. Well, Fort had an idea about cycles and events. Almost Spenglerian. He once said that when it's *steam-engine* time, people suddenly begin to *steam-engine*. Nothing much can be done to hasten that time. But, on the other hand, nothing much can be done to retard it. Maybe we all did the right thing because we recognized it was the right time."

I was back out on the street, looking up at the sky. And Walter Harland was back in his shop, looking at the ceiling. Or was it the ceiling?

4

LET'S save the rest for the kindergarten class. I found Peggy Dorr in Pasadena. Danny Keene had a boat at Balboa. Tom Humphrey – of all people! – operated a TV service repair shop not far from Farmer's Market.

And you know what else I found when I found them. Too-young faces, too-evasive answers, too-uniform a story. And that faraway look in their eyes.

It all added up to one big puzzle. unfortunately, detective stories aren't my line. I was out after stories which I couldn't get. The whole assignment was turning out to be one grand and glorious fiasco.

Where was the drama in it, the old heart-throb, the pathos, the violin-music in the background? Everything stopped for them in 1930, and the whole story belonged in the era before then when they made – literally *made* – the movies.

And nobody cared about *that* any more.

Or – did they?

Riding back from the visit with Tom Humphrey, the notion hit me.

By Louis B. Mayer and all the saints, here was a story! Not a lousy article, or a series of articles. *This* was a movie!

Look at how they flocked to the Jolson pictures, the life of Will Rogers, and all these phoney stage biography films. What about using the same gimmick on the life of Jeffrey Franklin? The whole silent-picture story, in glorious Technicolour, Warnercolour, Cinecolour, who cares?

Sure, Twentieth did *Hollywood Cavalcade*, but that was over twenty years ago. And besides, I had the kicker. Call it coincidence, fate, or just happy accident for the benefit of yours truly, I had something that would really sell such a film. No more working with imitators and phoneys – with the aid of a little modern lighting and make-up, the film could actually be done with the original cast playing real-life roles!

Natural. Socko. Boffo. The whole *Variety* lexicon flashed through my mind, and then the plot started to take shape, and before I knew it I was sitting at the typewriter banging out a treatment.

It was a good treatment. I didn't have to take my word for it. I had Cy Charney's word for it. Sat in his office and braved the blasts fired by two complete cigars as he read through it – then had the satisfaction of seeing one of the biggest agents on the Strip going crazy over my idea.

"I can place this one tomorrow," he said. "It's completely

copasetic. Of course you're not a name, but the idea is big enough. I think I can start the bidding at – lemme see now – thirty-four Gs. And maybe a writing assist for you on the real script. You free to take an assignment, boy?"

I damn' near broke my neck nodding.

"Keep in touch," said Charney. "Now get outta here and let me use my fine Eyetalian hand on this deal."

I got out of there, but things were happening so fast I couldn't quite believe my ears. Then again, I wasn't depending on my ears in this deal. I had Mr. Charney's fine Eyetalian hand.

And what a fine hand it was, too! He called me exactly twenty-six hours later. "All sewed," he said. "Freeman is crazy about it, and Jack wants it too. And I can get fifty from one of them if the other knows he's got competition. I'll have a contract in my office before the week is out. Can you line them up by that time?"

"Line who up?"

"The cast, boy! Old Franklin and Harland and the rest. I'm taking your say-so on this that they're still what you say they are instead of strictly for the glue-factory. Of course, they'll have to be tested and all, but I'm selling the story that they're still full of p. and v. Right? Now I'm asking you to line 'em up. Course, if you want me to come with you and put on the old pressure – "

"No, that won't be necessary," I cut in. "Let me handle it."

"Tell 'em not to worry about figures," Charney said. "I'll represent 'em – and they oughta know what that means in this town. And say, be sure you wangle a release out of old Franklin. It isn't exactly his life-story, but it's close enough so maybe you gotta cut him in on the story price. You work it out with him, huh?"

"Yes," I said. "I'll work it out with him."

But as I hung up, I wondered. I sat back and glanced up at the ceiling. There was no answer up there – not for me.

But then, I wasn't superstitious. Maybe that was the answer – actors were superstitious. Actors were superstitious, actors were always "on," actors were always hams.

Hams! I had it.

First thing I did, I sent a copy of the treatment, marked *PERSONAL*, to everybody I'd interviewed. Sent it Special Delivery, with an accompanying confidential letter. Gave it the complete buildup, including what a wonderful opportunity this would be to recreate the real art of the motion picture as it existed in the old days. I also hinted (and hoped I could actually make good on it, too) that a portion of the film's profits might be donated to the welfare funds for the benefit of less fortunate old-timers. And – in each letter – I stressed what a tremendous part was waiting for the recipient.

I gave the deal just twenty-four hours to get rolling. Then I went around to Walter Harland's bookshop.

The first thing I noticed as I came in was that he didn't wear his glasses any more. And he had on a suit that had nothing in it to attract or impress the bibliophile. He'd sharpened up. And that was fine.

"Well?" I said.

"Congratulations. It's tremendous. I had no idea what was in back of all this – your phoney interview approach fooled me completely."

He not only offered, he ushered me, to a chair. And pushed a package of Players my way. "Did me good to read it," he said. "I feel twenty years younger."

"You look it," I told him, truthfully. "And that's what a new generation of movie fans are going to say when they see you on the screen."

He beamed. "Danny and Tom called me last night. And Lucas – remember him? Used to do the heavies, with the long cigarette-holder, the sideburns and all? They're so excited – "

Something small stumbled into the bookshop; something old and withered and trembling like autumn's last leaf. It had a piping whisky tenor, and it bleated, "Walt, I dowanna in'errupt you, but I just gotta talk t'you a minute."

"Sure, Tiny." Harland got up, walked over to counter. The little man bleated in his ear for a moment. Harland went to the cash-register, rang up a NO SALE, and palmed something in the rummy's hand. "Now, if you'll excuse me – "

"Yeah, Walt. Yeah. God bless you." And autumn's last leaf blew away.

"Sorry." Harland came up to me, smiling.

"You don't have to be sorry."

"Yes I do."

"Meaning?"

"I can't do it. We can't do it. Your picture."

"But – "

"Spare me the sales-talk. You know I'm dying to do it. So are the others. I wouldn't fool you. Why, it would be like starting life all over again. What I wouldn't give to see my name up there, show all these young punks how a real actor can project."

"Then why – "

He was on stage and it was his scene all the way. "Because I told you we agreed to quit, all of us. And we did. There were one or two exceptions, but they aren't around any more. You didn't know it, but you just caught a glimpse of somebody who tried the other way. He only did one job for Franklin, and it was a minor comedy role, so I guess he got off easy in consequence. But it's no go. We couldn't take the risk."

"What risk?" I argued. "It's bound to be a smash. You can't lose a thing, and look what you stand to gain."

He shook his head. "Remember what I said about *steam-engine* time? We're horse-and-buggy people. And we've got to stay where we belong." He smiled, because he was doing *Pagliacci* now. "Besides, here's one thing you can bet on. There's no picture without the old man, and he'll never go for it. Never."

I shrugged myself out of the store, fast. I had a reason. I was looking for the last leaf. I knew him now – Tiny Collins. Never a big-name comic, but an old reliable. On a par with Heinee Mann, Billy Bevan, Jack Duffy.

One look at him, and at the little act he'd put on with Harland in the store, and I could figure out where to find him. It was just four doors down the street.

He was up there at the end of the bar, all alone with a small shot and a large beer for company. He'd stopped trembling, now that he was back home again.

I uttered the magic formula. "Aren't you Tiny Collins? I'll buy."

Just so happens that I was able to dredge up the names of several of his pictures. Just so happens that I was able to dredge up several more shots and beers. Just so happens that I got him into the back booth and steered the conversational boat into my particular idea of a snug harbour.

Tiny was funny. Drinking sobered him up. He stopped slurring his sentences and became thoughtful. I didn't mention the picture at all, but I did set the scene for him. I hinted that I might do an article on him, and that was enough. We were pals. And you can ask a pal anything, can't you?

"Level with me, now," I said. "What's got into all your old friends? Why are they so publicity-shy, and why did they quit?"

"You're asking me? Questions I been asking myself for twenty years – why they quit. Different with me. I got the

42

old axe. But they didn't have to quit. Seems like they all got together at once and decided."

"I know, Tiny. And I was wondering why. It just doesn't make sense."

"Nothin' makes sense," he agreed. "They wanna quit, so they get offers. I dowanna quit and right like that – snap! – I can't get a job. Me, Tiny Collins, that's played with Turpin and Fields and whatzisname and – "

"I know, Tiny. I know. Here, let's have another." We did, and I waited for the gulping to subside before I continued. "But surely you have a theory."

"Course I have a theory. Lotsa theories. First one is, they're all dead."

"Dead?"

"Sure. They got together and formed one of those – whatcha call 'em? – suicide pacts. When they heard about Blade and Terris and Ryan and Todd and all the others bumping at the same time, they figured they hadda go too. So they made an agreement and killed themselves." He meant to laugh, but midway it turned into a cough. I rode that one out, too.

"Only they're not dead, Tiny."

"What? Oh, sure. They're not dead. Only they look like they're dead. Didn't you notice? Now take me, frinstance. I'm same age as Tom Humphrey. But look at the difference. I'm all beat up and him – he looks just like he did in *The Black Tiger*. That was his last one, for First National 'r somebody. And all of them are alike. They look like they stopped when they stopped making pictures. Like they died and somebody embalmed 'em and wound 'em up."

I considered the theory for a moment. I also considered that Tiny's shot-and-beer routine might have something to do with the difference in appearances.

"You have any other theories?" I asked.

43

Tiny looked at me. That is, he made a good effort. But he was weaving again. "Yes. Yes, I got a theory. You won't tell anybody?"

"Honour bright."

"Good enough. Because – well, I know it sounds screwy. But I think they got scared." He groped for the beer-glass.

"Scared," I prompted.

"Good and scared. The old man, Franklin, he done it. He filled 'em full of the old juice. I heard stories. I ain't the one to confirm or deny. Confirm or deny." He liked the phrase.

"What stories?"

"The old man. He went off his trolley. After *Revolution*. And the talkies comin' in. And everybody croakin'. He got scared bad it might happen to him. And he – he was like God to the others. What he said – says – goes. He says quit, they quit. Also, you know how screwy they can get out here. Way I personally dope it out, maybe the old man he got roped into one of those phoney cults. You heard about phoney cults?"

I assured him I had heard plenty about phoney cults, all right.

"Suppose they got him and sold him a billa goods on one of them religious-like? And the high potentate or whoever said it's not in the cards for you to make pictures no more. It's not in the stars – "

Something clicked. *Stars. The ceiling.*

"Thanks, Tiny." I rose.

"Hey, where you goin'?"

"I've got a date."

"But I was just gettin' ready to buy a round – "

"Some other time. Thanks. Thanks very much." And I meant it.

I got out there and drove home. I drove slowly, because

I had a lot to think about. *In vino veritas*. Tiny made sense to me, at last.

Pieces began to form and fit together. I remembered a lot I'd forgotten about Jeffrey Franklin. His acknowledged superstitions. The way he'd hold up a scene for days until he got just the right actor for a walk-through bit. The way he'd junk whole sequences, just like Stroheim, because something didn't look *right*. The way he handled his actors; never cursing them, but praying for them instead. *Praying* for them. And (I remembered now) he had this trick of looking up in the air as if seeking divine guidance. Now just suppose he had been sneaking off to astrologers – Lord knows, plenty of them did in the old days and were still doing it today – and one of them gave him the word that Cancer was in Uranus or wherever. And stopped, just like that.

Could be. And could be, I might find out who his personal star-gazer was and make a little deal. Or switch him onto another astrological or half-astrological quack. It was a cinch I had to do something, and fast.

I got home, let myself in, and prepared to go to work. The astrologers had listings in the phone-book. I'd call every single one if necessary and –

It wasn't necessary. *My* phone rang instead. And the voice said:

"This is Jeffrey Franklin. I received your communication and I was wondering when I could see you."

"Why, tonight if you like, Mr. Franklin."

"Good. We have a lot to talk about. I'm going to do your picture."

5

WE sat in the suite, drinking scotch. The sun went down in the Pacific, courtesy M-G-M, and then Universal put the moon up in Technicolour.

Franklin did the talking. "So you see, it wasn't your story idea that convinced me, although I admit I was tempted. But when he called me up – the head of the studio, mind you! – and said his own car was on the way . . . "

I nodded, suddenly realizing that I'd underestimated Mr. Charney's fine Eyetalian hand.

" . . . and you can't imagine how it felt, just being back on a lot once more! Of course, many things are different, but I'm quite sure I have a grasp of technique. I've kept up on all the technical data – would you believe it, I still read every issue of *The American Cinematographer* – and I see everything that's released. And he has faith in me. He knows what it means to have me back in the Industry, actually directing – "

"Directing?"

"Certainly!" Franklin's smile outshone the moon. "That's the biggest surprise of all. I'm to direct as well as act in my own story."

What a fine Eyetalian hand!

There was no mistaking what this meant to Franklin. He was drunk on his own adrenalin. "I never realized they still remembered me," he said. "Of course, there was this Academy dinner thing, a few years ago, but I thought that was merely a gesture. And then, today, sitting there in the Executive Office, with everybody on the lot – I mean just that, everybody of any importance – literally begging to get in and meet me! You can't begin to realize what it means, son. You get used to the idea that it's all over, you even think of yourself as a has-been." He sighed. "But I'm ready, now. For the first time in years, I'm being honest with myself when I say I've always been ready. And I think, working together, all of us, that we can come up with a few tricks that will surprise the Industry."

Intoxication is contagious. I began to get a little high myself now. Fifty thousand less ten per cent is forty thousand, knock off half for taxes and it's still twenty thousand clear, plus an assist on the screenplay – Franklin would go to bat for me on that, I knew – and I'd be working on an A-budget special, and who knows where it might lead to? Three cheers for the *Grand Old-Timers!* Yes, and three cheers for –

The phone rang. Jeffrey Franklin walked over and picked it up in that very special way, the graceful actor's way. And his inflection, his modulation, was impeccable. "Yes, this is Jeffrey Franklin speaking."

I watched him do the scene, noted the sudden faltering, the sag. "No . . . not really . . . terrible . . . when? . . . of course, certainly, anything you think he needs . . . Friday afternoon, yes . . . where will it be? . . . yes . . . tomorrow . . . thanks."

The phone clicked. Franklin sat down. For a moment he almost looked his age. "Bad news," he said. "An old friend of mine was killed early this evening, in an accident. He was run over by a truck. The funeral will be Friday afternoon, and of course I'll attend. Our studio conference must be delayed until Monday." He shook his head. "It's hard to see them go, one by one," he mused. "You'll understand that, son, when you're my age."

"I'm sorry," I said. "Was it anyone I know?"

"I don't think so. Just somebody from the old days. He once did a bit in one of my productions. Tiny Collins."

This was my cue. I took it and kept my mouth shut. I kept it shut after I'd left Franklin, kept it shut all the next day. Of course there was a meeting with the gleeful Mr. Charney, during which he paced the floor and waved both of his fine Eyetalian hands in ecstasy over our good fortune. But I kept away from Harland and the others. They mustn't know that I'd talked to Tiny Collins. They mustn't know what I was beginning to suspect – because I didn't want to admit it, even to myself.

But Friday afternoon was the time set for the funeral, and I was there. And so was Danny Keene and Peggy Dorr and Tom Humphrey and Walter Harland and four other people whose names I never did learn. The local press and the *Reporter* had inserted routine squibs; but Tiny Collins, alive or dead, wasn't news. He wasn't even a *Grand Old-Timer,* or the studios would have sent flowers, charged off to the p-r fund.

I sat with Jeffrey Franklin as the hired reverend went through the stock routine with the assistance of the hired undertaker and the hired pallbearers. It was a poor performance. Two of the four strangers present were fat old ladies and they cried the way fat old ladies cry – loudly and the lighting was inferior – the kind rented by a quickie and unconvincingly. The cheap chapel set looked as though it might be stuck right in the middle of the scene, unit on a *per diem* basis.

And that was the kind of funeral accorded Tiny Collins who had played with Turpin and with Fields and with whatzisname, who had literally sunk to the gutter and was now making his final comeback, playing his one big scene as the star of the show. Too bad it was such a turkey. He wouldn't have approved.

The organist did routine things – why did that remind me so strongly of the old silents? – as we filed out. We had to finish the production at the cemetery.

It didn't take long. The sky was overcast, and the coming storm was so obvious that even the Chamber of Commerce would have scuttled for cover. The reverend mumbled his lines, performed his inevitable gestures, and then they lowered the body. It was a single take and they muffed it – let it down too fast. But nobody seemed to mind. Everyone started walking back to the path. The little group broke up, everybody seeking his car and eyeing the clouds whirling in from the west.

I stuck close to Jeffrey Franklin. Both of us had been pretty quiet throughout. He strode along the path, puffing on his pipe, and as I followed I realized he wasn't joining the group at the cars.

We walked over a little knoll into another part of the cemetery. There were more trees here, and plenty of monuments. A turn in the path took us into the exclusive residential district – for every cemetery out here has its own miniature Beverly Hills.

He climbed another knoll. There was a stone bench on top; a stone bench facing an imposing monument which featured a D'Artagan figure heroically poised atop a marble globe.

I looked twice at the figure, and recognition came to me before I read the name.

"Roland Blade!" I said.

"Yes." Jeffrey Franklin sat down on the stone bench facing the monument. He refilled his pipe as I joined him. The wind whistled through the treetops and I didn't like the tune.

This was the time to use the old psychology. I felt the need of a fine Eyetalian hand of my own – to grab Franklin by the scruff of his neck and raise his spirits. Not knowing exactly how to do it, or what to say, I blurted out what was on my mind.

"The funeral certainly wasn't much of a production, was it?"

He shrugged. "Why should it be? Tiny wasn't important enough to be worthy of a script. The whole scene was done off the cuff."

That was odd. He must have been thinking the same way I was — comparing the funeral to a motion picture. I remembered his comment on the *Restlawn* nurse, and his references to "type-casting." Peculiar.

"Look, son," said Franklin. "I'd better talk to you."

"Go right ahead. It won't rain for a while."

Depends on the script."

"What scripts?"

Franklin emptied his pipe. "That's what I'm going to tell you. It isn't easy, but now that we're going ahead with the movie, you'll be a part of things, whether you like it or not. And the chances are, you won't like it. I don't."

I steadied myself (here it comes, boy, here's your astrology or whatever it is, and you'd better not argue or laugh in his face.)

"Omar Khayyam must have known when he wrote those lines about a chess game. In Omar's time it might have been chess. Shakespeare put it down when he said, 'All the world's a stage.' And perhaps it was a stage when he lived. For us, it's motion picture production. *Steam-engine* time. *Movie* time. And it amuses them to write a script, cast it, produce and direct."

He paused, just long enough for me to say, *"Them?"*

"Them. They. It. One or many. Call the forces what you will — gods, demons, Fates, or cosmic intelligences. All I know is that *they* exist, have always existed, will always exist. And it amuses them to select certain mortals to enact roles in the little dramas they devise."

I forgot my good resolutions and burst out, "Are you trying to tell me that the whole world is being run as a movie-plot, with some super-human forces directing everyone's actions?"

He shook his head. "Not everyone's. Just a few, a select few. The superior ones, and those brought into contact with them by the necessity of the plot. Omar must have known, Shakespeare must have known, for they were superior. The majority of mankind goes along, 'shooting off the cuff' and conducting affairs in the usual shoddy, shabby manner. Even their crimes, their love-affairs, their deaths are undramatic and unconvincing. Their lines are pedestrian and uninspired, and they never *create*.

"Don't you see it now? That's the whole criterion – if you're creative, you have some affinity with *them. They* notice you and write you into the script. You spoke of me, and some of the others, as being dream-makers. We are. We were, rather, in the old days, because it was part of the plot."

The wind was roaring in from the ocean, but it didn't bother me any longer. I had other things to worry about, now. Franklin was batty, and –

"I wish I could get you to understand," he said. "Because it's really quite important, you know. Once you accept the fact, you'll learn how to adjust. You won't make the mistake of going against the Producer or the Director or the Writer. You won't run the risk of being edited or cut out of the film. Because you're an actor now, like it or not. And you can't fight the script. If you do the Director will catch you. And he'll have the Cutter slice your scenes. That's what happened to Blade, and a lot of the others."

You can't reason with a loony, but I tried. "Look, Mr. Franklin – you just aren't getting through to me. You sound more like Tiny Collins the other night, when he –"

It slipped out, just like that. (Was it *supposed* to, *was* it in the script?)

"You knew Tiny Collins?"

"Well, I talked to him." And I told him what had happened. He listened, shaking his head. He glanced up at the sky, at the scudding clouds. Was he waiting for another cue before he spoke?

"Then perhaps Tiny's accident wasn't an – accident. He got back in the script again."

"Please, Mr. Franklin. I wish you wouldn't talk that way. This idea that all the important people in the world are part of some cosmic movie just doesn't make sense."

"What does make sense?" he shot back. "World wars, atom-bombs, plagues, famines? Perhaps it isn't a movie for everyone, just for the movie-makers. Maybe *they* play War up there for generals and statesmen. And *others* might run a Business for executives. If you ever get to know any military leaders or high politicians or industrial tycoons, you might ask them. If it's true, they'll know. They'll find out – when they try to drop the script, run their own show."

A punctuation of distant thunder.

"Omar knew. He wrote what he was supposed to write – perhaps that's why *they* do it, *they* might feed on creative energy in some way we'll never comprehend – and then he stopped. Never wrote another line but retired to obscurity. Because *they* tired of the scene and set a new one *Rubaiyat-time* was over. And Shakespeare stopped writing, too. Think about it for a while; think of the names, the big names, who flourished for a given period and then dropped out of the picture forever. They were still at the height of their powers, too."

I tried to use logic. "But think of all the others who have kept going," I said. "The thousands who didn't quit."

"Some of them weren't big enough to be directed," Franklin answered. "Some of them undoubtedly knew, but were defiant. Napoleon's script ended at Elba, but he was greater than the Producer. He came back. Well, you don't make come-backs in this world. They end in disaster. *Napoleon-time* was over. He held out for exactly one hundred days."

The sky was dark. Franklin lit his pipe and a thousand tiny red eyes winked out in the wind. "But I'm not talking theory, son. I'm talking reality. I'm talking about myself, and my company, and a dozen others who must have learned the secret in the days when we made the silent dreams. The script was right for us to succeed, then, and our success was sudden and spectacular. That was *silent-time*. But *talkie-time* came, and there was a new script, calling for new players. We had our choice; get out or be cut out. The wise ones retired. The Cutter got the rest. Now do you see?"

I saw. "Maybe you're right. But – why are you telling me this."

Franklin smiled It was a ghost-smile in ghost-light, but I sensed it. "Because in the last few days I've found out that I'm more than an actor. I'm a man. And a man must lead his own life. I thought, at one time, that I could take my bow and sit in the audience for the rest of the show. And for more than twenty years, I did.

"Then you came along, with your script. Your script, not *theirs*. And I want to do it. I want to direct it. I'm a director, too."

"Good." And it *was* good, I thought. "Then we'll do the picture."

He patted my shoulder. "Of course we will, son. But it wouldn't be fair to go ahead without warning you. There's the Cutters to consider. If the Director spots us ad-libbing and raises his finger –"

So help me, the old ham lifted his own finger and pointed dramatically at the statue of Roland Blade. And the thunder came booming in, right on cue.

For a moment, there, he almost had me sold. I thought of Blade, of Fay Terris, Matty Ryan and all the others who defied the coming of sound, who died before their time, died in sudden and inexplicable violence. Died before their time? No! *Cut off* before their time. Or, *cut off after* their time.

I wondered if *they* were watching us now, listening in on the scene, appreciating the gestures. I wondered if *they* had just sent out a signal to turn on the rain-making machine.

The downpour came. I rose hastily from the bench, expecting Jeffrey Franklin to join me.

"In a minute," he said. "I'm just – thinking –"

"Now, look," I called. "You promised."

Jeffrey Franklin straightened up. He stood there in the rain, legs apart, feet firmly planted, chin jutting forth aggressively.

"You have my word," he called. "I promised you, I promised myself, and I promise *them*. From now on, I direct and act my own life. I'll make the picture."

I was a hundred feet away, the night was dark, and the rain a deluge; but even so, I caught his face. The chin was tilting up, now. Jeffrey Franklin was staring at the sky again.

Then it happened.

It was lightning of course; a single, sharp bolt that chopped down Jeffrey Franklin and the picture, my hopes, everything. As the papers said later, and as I desperately told myself over and over again, even as I ran towards the dismembered corpse, it was only a freak accident.

But I couldn't hide from myself, as I ran, the final revelation or realization. Oh, it was a lightning-bolt, all right – but to me, in the single instant that I saw it, it was more like the sharp blade of a gigantic scissors.

Yours Truly, Jack the Ripper

I LOOKED at the stage Englishman. He looked at me.

"Sir Guy Hollis?" I asked.

"Indeed. Have I the pleasure of addressing John Carmody, the psychiatrist?"

I nodded.My eyes swept over the figure of my distinguished visitor. Tall, lean, sandy-haired – with the traditional tufted moustache. And the tweeds. I suspected a monocle concealed in a vest pocket, and wondered if he'd left his umbrella in the outer office.

But more than that, I wondered what the devil had impelled Sir Guy Hollis of the British Embassy to seek out a total stranger here in Chicago.

Sir Guy didn't help matters any as he sat down. He cleared his throat, glanced around nervously, tapped his pipe against the side of the desk. Then he opened his mouth.

"Mr. Carmody," he said, "have you ever heard of – Jack the Ripper?"

"The murderer?" I asked.

"Exactly. The greatest monster of them all. Worse than Springheel Jack or Crippen. Jack the Ripper. Red Jack."

"I've heard of him," I said.

"Do you know his history?"

"Listen, Sir Guy," I muttered. "I don't think we'll get any place swapping old wives' tales about famous crimes of history."

Another bulls-eye. He took a deep breath.

"This is no old wives' tale. It's a matter of life or death."

He was so wrapped up in his obsession he even talked that way. Well – I was willing to listen. We psychiatrists get paid for listening.

"Go ahead," I told him. "Let's have the story."

Sir Guy lit a cigarette and began to talk.

"London, 1888," he began. "Late summer and early fall. That was the time. Out of nowhere came the shadowy figure of Jack the Ripper – a stalking shadow with a knife, prowling through London's East End. Haunting the squalid dives of Whitechapel, Spitalfields. Where he came from no one knew. But he brought death. Death in a knife.

"Six times that knife descended to slash the throats and bodies of London's women. Drabs and alley sluts. August 7th was the date of the first butchery. They found her body lying there with 39 stab wounds. A ghastly murder. On August 31st, another victim. The press became interested. The slum inhabitants were more deeply interested still.

"Who was this unknown killer who prowled in their midst and struck at will in the deserted alley-ways of night-town? And what was more important – when would he strike again?

"September 8th was the date. Scotland Yard assigned special deputies. Rumours ran rampant. The atrocious nature of the slayings was the subject for shocking speculation.

"The killer used a knife – expertly. He cut throats and removed – certain portions – of the bodies after death. He chose victims and settings with a fiendish deliberation. No one saw him or heard him. But watchmen making their grey round in the dawn would stumble across the hacked and horrid thing that was the Ripper's handiwork.

"Who was he? What was he? A mad surgeon? A butcher? An insane scientist? A pathological degenerate escaped from an asylum? A deranged nobleman? A member of the London police?

"Then the poem appeared in the newspapers. The anonymous poem, designed to put a stop to speculations – but which only aroused public interest to a further frenzy. A mocking little stanza:

> I'm not a butcher, I'm not a Yid
> Nor yet a foreign skipper,
> But I'm your own true loving friend,
> Yours truly – Jack the Ripper.

"And on September 30th, two more throats were slashed open."

I interrupted Sir Guy for a moment.

"Very interesting," I commented. I'm afraid a faint hint of sarcasm crept into my voice.

He winced, but didn't falter in his narrative.

"There was silence, then, in London for a time. Silence, and a nameless fear. When would Red Jack strike again? They waited through October. Every figment of fog concealed his phantom presence. Concealed it well – for nothing was learned of the Ripper's identity, or his purpose. The drabs of London shivered in the raw wind of early November. Shivered, and were thankful for the coming of each morning's sun.

"November 9th. They found her in her room. She lay there very quietly, limbs neatly arranged. And beside her, with equal neatness, were laid her head and heart. The Ripper had outdone himself in execution.

"Then, panic. But needless panic. For though press, police, and populace alike waited in sick dread, Jack the Ripper did not strike again.

"Months passed. A year. The immediate interest died, but not the memory. They said Jack had skipped to America. That he had committed suicide. They said – and they wrote. They've written ever since. Theories, hypotheses, arguments, treatises. But to this day no one knows who Jack the Ripper was. Or why he killed. Or why he stopped killing."

Sir Guy was silent. Obviously he expected some comment from me.

"You tell the story well," I remarked. "Though with a slight emotional bias."

"I've got all the documents," said Sir Guy Hollis. "I've made a collection of existing data and studied it."

I stood up. "Well," I yawned, in mock fatigue, "I've enjoyed your little bedtime story a great deal, Sir Guy. It was kind of you to abandon your duties at the British Embassy to drop in on a poor psychiatrist and regale him with your anecdotes."

Goading him always did the trick.

"I suppose you want to know why I'm interested?" he snapped.

"Yes. That's exactly what I'd like to know. Why are you interested?"

"Because," said Sir Guy Hollis, "I am on the trail of Jack the Ripper now. I think he's here – in Chicago!"

I sat down again. This time I did the blinking act.

"Say that again," I stuttered.

"Jack the Ripper is alive, in Chicago, and I'm out to find him."

"Wait a minute," I said. "Wait–a–minute!"

He wasn't smiling. It wasn't a joke.

"See here," I said. "What was the date of these murders?"

"August to November, 1888."

"1888? But if Jack the Ripper was an able-bodied man in 1888, he'd surely be dead today! Why look, man – if he were merely born in that year, he'd be 57 years old today!"

"Would he?" smiled Sir Guy Hollis. "Or should I say 'Would she?' Because Jack the Ripper may have been a woman. Or any number of things."

"Sir Guy," I said. "You came to the right person when you looked me up. You definitely need the services of a psychiatrist."

"Perhaps. Tell me, Mr. Carmody, do you think I'm crazy?"

I looked at him and shrugged. But I had to give him a truthful answer.

"Frankly – no."

"Then you might listen to the reasons I believe Jack the Ripper is alive today."

"I might."

"I've studied these cases for thirty years. Been over the actual ground. Talked to officials. Talked to friends and acquaintances of the poor drabs who were killed. Visited with men and women in the neighbourhood. Collected an entire library of material touching on Jack the Ripper. Studied all the wild theories or crazy notions.

"I learned a little. Not much, but a little. I won't bore you with my conclusions. But there was another branch of inquiry that yielded more fruitful return. I have studied unsolved crimes. Murders.

"I could show you clippings from the papers of half the world's great cities. San Francisco. Shanghai. Calcutta. Omsk. Paris. Berlin. Pretoria. Cairo. Milan. Adelaide.

"The trail is there, the pattern. Unsolved crimes. Slashed throats of women. With the peculiar disfigurations and removals. Yes, I've followed a trail of blood. From New York westwards across the continent. Then to the Pacific. From there to Africa. During the World War of 1914-18 it was Europe. After that, South America. And since 1930, the United States again. Eighty-seven such murders – and to the trained criminologist, all bear the stigma of the Ripper's handiwork.

"Recently there were the so-called Cleveland torso slayings. Remember? A shocking series. And finally, two recent deaths in Chicago. Within the past six months. One out on South Dearborn. The other somewhere up on Halsted. Same type of crime, same technique. I tell you, there are unmistakable indications in all these affairs – indications of the work of Jack the Ripper!"

I smiled.

"A very tight theory," I said. "I'll not question your evidence at all, or the deductions you draw. You're the criminologist, and I'll take your word for it. Just one thing remains to be explained. A minor point, perhaps, but worth mentioning."

"And what is that?" asked Sir Guy.

"Just how could a man of, let us say, 85 years commit these crimes? For if Jack the Ripper was around 30 in 1888 and lived, he'd be 85 today."

Sir Guy Hollis was silent. I had him there. But –

"Suppose he didn't get any older?" whispered Sir Guy.

"What's that?"

"Suppose Jack the Ripper didn't grow old? Suppose he is still a young man today?"

"All right," I said. "I'll suppose for a moment. Then I'll stop supposing and call for my nurse to restrain you."

"I'm serious," said Sir Guy.

"They all are," I told him. "That's the pity of it all, isn't it? They know they hear voices and see demons. But we lock them up just the same."

It was cruel, but it got results. He rose and faced me.

"It's a crazy theory, I grant you," he said. "All the theories about the Ripper are crazy. The idea that he was a doctor. Or a maniac. Or a woman. The reasons advanced for such beliefs are flimsy enough. There's nothing to go by. So why should my notion be any worse?"

"Because people grow older," I reasoned with him. "Doctors, maniacs, and women alike."

"What about – *sorcerers*?"

"Sorcerers?"

"Necromancers. Wizards. Practicers of Black Magic?"

"What's the point?"

"I studied," said Sir Guy. "I studied everything. After awhile I began to study the dates of the murders. The pattern those dates formed. The rhythm. The solar, lunar, stellar rhythm. The sidereal aspect. The astrological significance."

He was crazy. But I still listened.

"Suppose Jack the Ripper didn't murder for murder's sake alone? Suppose he wanted to make – a sacrifice?"

"What kind of a sacrifice?"

Sir Guy shrugged. "It is said that if you offer blood to the dark gods they grant boons. Yes, if a blood offering is made at the proper time – when the moon and the stars are right – and with the proper ceremonies – they grant boons. Boons of youth. Eternal youth."

"But that's nonsense!"

"No. That's – Jack the Ripper."

I stood up. "A most interesting theory," I told him. "But Sir Guy – there's just one thing I'm interested in. Why do you come here and tell it to me? I'm not an authority on witchcraft. I'm not a police official or criminologist. I'm a practising psychiatrist. What's the connection?"

Sir Guy smiled.

"You are interested, then?"

"Well, yes. There must be some point."

"There is. But I wished to be assured of your interest first. Now I can tell you my plan."

"And just what is that plan?"

Sir Guy gave me a long look. Then he spoke.

"John Carmody," he said, "you and I are going to capture Jack the Ripper."

2

THAT'S the way it happened. I've given the gist of that first interview in all its intricate and somewhat boring detail, because I think it's important. It helps to throw some light on Sir Guy's character and attitude. And in view of what happened after that –

But I'm coming to those matters.

Sir Guy's thought was simple. It wasn't even a thought. Just a hunch.

"You know the people here," he told me. "I've inquired. That's why I came to you as the ideal man for my purpose. You number amongst your acqaintances many writer's, painters, poets. The so-called intelligentsia. The Bohemians. The lunatic fringe from the near north side.

"For certain reasons – never mind what they are – my clues lead me to infer that Jack the Ripper is a member of that element. He chooses to pose as an eccentric. I've a feeling that with you to take me around and introduce me to your set, I might hit upon the right person."

"It's all right with me," I said. "But just how are you going to look for him? As you say, he might be anybody, anywhere. And you have no idea what he looks like. He might be young or old. Jack the Ripper – a Jack of all trades? Rich man, poor man, beggar man, thief, doctor, lawyer – how will you know?"

"We shall see," Sir Guy sighed heavily. "But I must find him at once."

"Why the hurry?"

Sir Guy sighed again. "Because in two days he will kill again."

"Are you sure?"

"Sure as the stars. I've plotted this chart, you see. All of the murders correspond to certain astrological rhythm patterns. If, as I suspect, he makes a blood sacrifice to renew his youth, he must murder within two days. Notice the pattern of his first crimes in London. August 7th. Then August 31. September 8th. September 30th. November 9th. Intervals of 24 days, 9 days, 22 days – he killed two this time – and then 40 days. Of course there were crimes in between. There had to be. But they weren't discovered and pinned on him.

"At any rate, I've worked out a pattern for him, based on all my data. And I say that within the next two days he kills. So I must seek him out, somehow, before then."

"And I'm still asking you what you want me to do."

"Take me out," said Sir Guy. "Introduce me to your friends. Take me to parties."

"But where do I begin? As far as I know, my artistic friends, despite the eccentricities, are all normal people."

"So is the Ripper. Perfectly normal. Except on certain nights." Again that far-away look in Sir Guy's eyes. "Then he becomes an ageless pathological monster, crouching to kill, on evenings when the stars blaze down in the blazing patterns of death."

"All right," I said. "All right. I'll take you to parties, Sir Guy. I want to go myself, anyway. I need the drinks they'll serve there, after listening to your kind of talk."

We made our plans. And that evening I took him over to Lester Baston's studio.

As we ascended to the penthouse roof in the elevator I took the opportunity to warn Sir Guy.

"Baston's a real screwball," I cautioned him. "So are

64

his guests. Be prepared for anything and everything."

"I am." Sir Guy Hollis was perfectly serious. He put his hand in his trousers pocket and pulled out a gun.

"What the –" I began.

"If I see him I'll be ready," Sir Guy said. He didn't smile, either.

"But you can't go running around at a party with a loaded revolver in your pocket, man!"

"Don't worry, I won't behave foolishly."

I wondered. Sir Guy Hollis was not, to my way of thinking, a normal man.

We stepped out of the elevator, went towards Baston's apartment door.

"By the way," I murmured, "just how do you wish to be introduced? Shall I tell them who you are and what you are looking for?"

"I don't care. Perhaps it would be best to be frank."

"But don't you think that the Ripper – if by some miracle he or she is present – will immediately get the wind up and take cover?"

"I think the shock of the announcement that I am hunting the Ripper would provoke some kind of betraying gesture on his part," said Sir Guy.

"You'd make a pretty good psychiatrist yourself," I conceded. "It's a fine theory. But I warn you, you're going to be in for a lot of ribbing. This is a wild bunch."

Sir Guy smiled.

"I'm ready," he announced. "I have a little plan of my own. Don't be shocked at anything I do," he warned me.

I nodded and knocked on the door.

Baston opened it and poured out into the hall. His eyes were as red as the maraschino cherries in his Manhattan. He teetered back and forth regarding us very gravely. He squinted at my square-cut homburg hat and Sir Guy's moustache.

"Aha," he intoned. "The Walrus and the Carpenter."

I introduced Sir Guy.

"Welcome," said Baston, gesturing us inside with over elaborate courtesy. He stumbled after us into the garish parlour.

I stared at the crowd that moved restlessly through the fog of cigarette smoke.

It was the shank of the evening for this mob. Every hand held a drink. Every face held a slightly hectic flush. Over in one corner the piano was going full blast, but the imperious strains of the *March* from *The Love for Three Oranges* couldn't drown out the profanity from the crap-game in the other corner.

Prokofieff had no chance against African polo, and one set of ivories rattled louder than the other.

Sir Guy got a monocle-full right away. He saw LaVerne Gonnister, the poetess, hit Hymie Kralik in the eye. He saw Hymie sit down on the floor and cry until Dick Pool accidentally stepped on his stomach as he walked through to the dining room for a drink.

He heard Nadia Vilinoff the commercial artist tell Johnny Odcutt that she thought his tatooing was in dreadful taste, and he saw Barclay Melton crawl under the dining room table with Johnny Odcutt's wife.

His zoological observations might have continued indefinitely if Lester Baston hadn't stepped to the centre of the room and called for silence by dropping a vase on the floor.

"We have distinguished visitors in our midst," bawled Lester, waving his empty glass in our direction. "None other than the Walrus and the Carpenter. The Walrus is Sir Guy Hollis, a something-or-other from the British Embassy. The Carpenter, as you all know, is our own John Carmody, the prominent dispenser of libido liniment."

He turned and grabbed Sir Guy by the arm, dragging

him to the middle of the carpet. For a moment I thought
Hollis might object, but a quick wink reassured me. He
was prepared for this.

"It is our custom, Sir Guy," said Baston, loudly, "to
subject our new friends to a little cross-examination. Just
a little formality at these very formal gatherings, you understand. Are you prepared to answer questions?"

Sir Guy nodded and grinned.

"Very well," Baston muttered. "Friends – I give you
this bundle from Britain. Your witness."

Then the ribbing started. I meant to listen, but at that
moment Lydia Dare saw me and dragged me off into the
vestibule for one of those Darling-I-waited-for-your-call-
all-day routines.

By the time I had got rid of her and went back, the
impromptu quiz session was in full swing. From the attitude of the crowd, I gathered that Sir Guy was doing all
right for himself.

Then Baston himself interjected a question that upset
the apple-cart.

"And what, may I ask, brings you to our midst tonight? What is your mission, oh Walrus?"

"I'm looking for Jack the Ripper."

Nobody laughed.

Perhaps it struck them all the way it did me. I glanced
at my neighbours and began to *wonder*.

LaVerne Gonnister. Hymie Kralik. Harmless. Dick
Pool. Nadia Vilinoff. Johnny Odcutt and his wife. Barclay
Melton. Lydia Dare. All harmless.

But what a forced smile on Dick Pool's face! And that
sly, self-conscious smirk that Barclay Melton wore!

Oh, it was absurd, I grant you. But for the first
time I saw these people in a new light. I wondered
about their lives – their secret lives beyond the scenes of
parties.

How many of them were playing a part, concealing something?

Who here would worship Hecate and grant that horrid goddess the dark boon of blood?

Even Lester Baston might be masquerading.

The mood was upon us all, for a moment. I saw questions flicker in the circle of eyes around the room.

Sir Guy stood there, and I could swear he was fully conscious of the situation he'd created, and enjoyed it.

I wondered idly just what was *really* wrong with him. Why he had this odd fixation concerning Jack the Ripper. Maybe he was hiding secrets, too . . .

Baston, as usual, broke the mood. He burlesqued it.

"The Walrus isn't kidding, friends," he said. He slapped Sir Guy on the back and put his arm around him as he orated. "Our English cousin is really on the trail of the fabulous Jack the Ripper. You all remember Jack the Ripper, I presume? Quite a cut-up in the old days, as I recall. Really had some ripping good times when he went out on a tear.

"The Walrus has some idea that the Ripper is still alive, probably prowling around Chicago with a Boy Scout knife. In fact – " Baston paused impressively and shot it out in a rasping stage-whisper – "in fact, he has reason to believe that Jack the Ripper might even be right here in our midst tonight."

There was the expected reaction of giggles and grins. Baston eyed Lydia Dare reprovingly. "You girls needn't laugh," he smirked. "Jack the Ripper might be a woman, too, you know Sort of Jill the Ripper."

"You mean you actually suspect one of us?" shrieked LaVerne Gonnister, simpering up to Sir Guy. "But that Jack the Ripper person disappeared ages ago, didn't he? In 1888?"

"Aha!" interrupted Baston. "How do you know so

much about it, young lady? Sounds suspicious! Watch her, Sir Guy – she may not be as young as she appears. These lady poets have dark pasts."

The tension was gone, the mood was shattered, and the whole thing was beginning to degenerate into a trivial party joke. The man who had played the *March* was eyeing the piano with a *Scherzo* gleam in his eye that augured ill for Prokofieff. Lydia Dare was glancing at the kitchen, waiting to make a break for another drink.

Then Baston caught it.

"Guess what?" he yelled. "The Walrus has a gun."

His embracing arm had slipped and encountered the hard outline of the gun in Sir Guy's pocket. He snatched it out before Hollis had the opportunity to protest.

I stared hard at Sir Guy, wondering if this thing had carried far enough. But he flicked a wink my way and I remembered he had told me not to be alarmed.

So I waited as Baston broached a drunken inspiration.

"Let's play fair with our friend the Walrus," he cried. "He came all the way from England to our party on this mission. If none of you is willing to confess, I suggest we give him a chance to find out – the hard way."

"What's up?" asked Johnny Odcutt.

"I'll turn out the lights for one minute. Sir Guy can stand here with his gun. If anyone in this room is the Ripper he can either run for it or take the opportunity to – well eradicate his pursuer. Fair enough?"

It was even sillier than it sounds, but it caught the popular fancy. Sir Guy's protest went unheard in the ensuing babble. And before I could stride over and put in my two cents' worth, Lester Baston had reached the light switch.

"Don't anybody move," he announced, with fake solemnity. "For one minute we will remain in darkness – perhaps at the mercy of the killer. At the end of that time,

I'll turn up the lights again and look for bodies. Choose your partners, ladies and gentlemen."

The lights went out.

Somebody giggled.

I heard footsteps in the darkness. Mutterings.

A hand brushed my face.

The watch on my wrist ticked violently. But even louder, rising above it, I heard another thumping. The beating of my heart. Absurd. Standing in the dark with a group of tipsy fools. And yet there was real terror lurking here, rustling through the velvet blackness.

Jack the Ripper prowled in darkness like this. And Jack the Ripper had a knife. Jack the Ripper had a madman's brain and madman's purpose.

But Jack the Ripper was dead, dead and dust these many years – by every human law.

Only there are no human laws when you feel yourself in the darkness, when the darkness hides and protects and and the outer mask slips off your face and you feel something welling up within you, a brooding shapeless purpose that is brother to the blackness.

Sir Guy Hollis shrieked.

There was a ghastly thud.

Baston had the lights on.

Everybody screamed.

Sir Guy Hollis lay sprawled on the floor in the centre of the room. The gun was still clutched in his hand.

I glanced at the faces, marvelling at the variety of expressions human beings can assume when confronting horror.

All the faces were present in the circle. Nobody had fled.

And yet Sir Guy Hollis lay there . . .

LaVerne Gonnister was wailing and hiding her face. "All right."

Sir Guy rolled over and jumped to his feet. He was smiling.

"Just an experiment, eh? If Jack the Ripper were among those present, and thought I had been murdered, he would have betrayed himself in some way when the lights went on and he saw me lying there.

"I am convinced of your individual and collective innocence. Just a gentle spoof, my friends."

Hollis stared at the goggling Baston and the rest of them crowding in behind.

"Shall we leave, John?" he called to me. "It's getting late, I think."

Turning, he headed for the closet. I followed him. Nobody said a word.

It was a pretty dull party after that.

3

I MET Sir Guy the following evening as we agreed, on the corner of 29th and South Halsted.

After what had happened the night before, I was prepared for almost anything. But Sir Guy seemed matter-of-fact enough as he stood huddled against a grimy doorway and waited for me to appear.

"Boo!" I said, jumping out suddenly. He smiled. Only the betraying gesture of his left hand indicated that he'd instinctively reached for his gun when I startled him.

"All ready for our wild goose chase?" I asked.

"Yes." He nodded. "I'm glad that you agreed to meet me without asking questions," he told me. "It shows you trust my judgement." He took my arm and edged me along the street slowly.

"It's foggy tonight, John," said Sir Guy Hollis. "Like London."

I nodded.

"Cold, too, for November."

I nodded again and half-shivered my agreement.

"Curious," mused Sir Guy. "London fog and November. The place and the time of the Ripper murders."

I grinned through darkness. "Let me remind you, Sir Guy, that this isn't London, but Chicago. And it isn't November, 1888. It's over fifty years later."

Sir Guy returned my grin, but without mirth. "I'm not so sure, at that," he murmured. "Look about you. Those tangled alleys and twisted streets. They're like the East End. Mitre Square. And surely they are as ancient as fifty years, at least."

"You're in the coloured neighbourhood off South Clarke Street," I said, shortly. "And why you dragged me down here I still don't know.

"It's a hunch," Sir Guy admitted. "Just a hunch on my part, John. I want to wander around down here. There's the same geographical conformation in these streets as in those courts where the Ripper roamed and slew. That's where we'll find him, John. Not in the bright lights of the Bohemian neighbourhood, but down here in the darkness. The darkness where he waits and crouches."

"Is that why you brought a gun?" I asked. I was unable to keep a trace of sarcastic nervousness from my voice. All of this talk, this incessant obsession with Jack the Ripper, got on my nerves more than I cared to admit.

"We may need a gun," said Sir Guy, gravely. "After all, tonight is the appointed night."

I sighed. We wandered on through the foggy, deserted streets. Here and there a dim light burned above a gin-mill doorway. Otherwise, all was darkness and shadow. Deep, gaping alleyways loomed as we proceeded down a slanting side-street.

We crawled through that fog, alone and silent, like two tiny maggots floundering within a shroud.

When that thought hit me, I winced. The atmosphere was beginning to get *me*, too. If I didn't watch my step I'd go as loony as Sir Guy.

"Can't you see there's not a soul around these streets?" I said, tugging at his coat impatiently.

"He's bound to come," said Sir Guy. "He'll be drawn here. This is what I've been looking for. A *genius loci*. An evil spot that attracts evil. Always, when he slays, it's in the slums.

"You see, that must be one of his weaknesses. He has a fascination for squalor. Besides, the women he needs for sacrifice are more easily found in the dives and stewpots of a great city."

I smiled. "Well, let's go into one of the dives or stewpots," I suggested. "I'm cold. Need a drink. This damned fog gets into your bones. You Britishers can stand it, but I like warmth and dry heat."

We emerged from our side-street and stood upon the threshold of an alley.

Through the white clouds of mist ahead, I discerned a dim blue light, a naked bulb dangling from a beer sign above an alley tavern.

"Let's take a chance," I said. "I'm beginning to shiver."

"Lead the way," said Sir Guy. I led him down the alley passage. We halted before the door of the dive.

"What are you waiting for?" he asked.

"Just looking in," I told him. "This is a tough neighbourhood, Sir Guy. Never know what you're liable to run into. And I'd prefer we didn't get into the wrong company. Some of these Negro places resent white customers."

"Good idea, John."

I finished my inspection through the doorway. "Looks deserted," I murmured. "Let's try it."

We entered a dingy bar. A feeble light flickered above the counter and railing, but failed to penetrate the further gloom of the back booths.

A gigantic Negro lolled across the bar – a black giant with prognathous jaw and ape-like torso. He scarcely stirred as we came in, but his eyes flicked open quite suddenly and I knew he noted our presence and was judging us.

"Evening," I said.

He took his time before replying. Still sizing us up. Then, he grinned.

"Evening, gents. What's your pleasure?"

"Gin," I said. "Two gins. It's a cold night."

"That's right, gents."

He poured, I paid, and took the glasses over to one of the booths. We wasted no time in emptying them. The fiery liquor warmed.

I went over to the bar and got the bottle. Sir Guy and I poured ourselves another drink. The big Negro went back into his doze, with one wary eye half-open against any sudden activity.

The clock over the bar ticked on. The wind was rising outside, tearing the shroud of fog to ragged shreds. Sir Guy and I sat in the warm booth and drank our gin.

He began to talk, and the shadows crept up about us to listen.

He rambled a great deal. He went over everything he'd said in the office when I met him, just as though I hadn't heard it before. The poor devils with obsessions are like that.

I listened very patiently. I poured Sir Guy another drink. And another.

But the liquor only made him more talkative. How he did run on! About ritual killings and prolonging the life unnaturally – the whole fantastic tale came out again. And of course, he maintained his unyielding conviction that the Ripper was abroad tonight.

I suppose I was guilty of goading him.

"Very well," I said, unable to keep the impatience from my voice. "Let us say that your theory is correct – even though we must overlook every natural law and swallow a lot of superstition to give it any credence.

"But let us say, for the sake of argument, that you are right. Jack the Ripper was a man who discovered how to prolong his own life through making human sacrifices. He did travel around the world as you believe. He is in Chicago now and he is planning to kill. In other words, let us suppose that everything you claim is gospel truth. So what?"

"What do you mean, 'so what'?" said Sir Guy.

"I mean – so what?" I answered. "If all this is true, it still doesn't prove that by sitting down in a dingy gin-mill on the South Side, Jack the Ripper is going to walk in here and let you kill him, or turn him over to the police. And come to think of it, I don't even know now just what you intend to *do* with him if you ever did find him."

Sir Guy gulped his gin. "I'd capture the bloody swine," he said. "Capture him and turn him over to the government, together with all the papers and documentary evidence I've collected against him over a period of many years. I've spent a fortune investigating this affair, I tell you, a fortune! His capture will mean the solution of hundreds of unsolved crimes, of that I am convinced.

"I tell you, a mad beast is loose on this world! An ageless, eternal beast, sacrificing to Hecate and the dark gods!"

In vino veritas. Or was all this babbling the result of too much gin? It didn't matter. Sir Guy Hollis had another. I sat there and wondered what to do with him. The man was rapidly working up to a climax of hysterical drunkenness.

"One other point," I said, more for the sake of conversation than in the hopes of obtaining information. "You still don't explain how it is that you hope to just blunder into the Ripper."

"He'll be around," said Sir Guy. "I'm psychic. I know."

Sir Guy wasn't psychic. He was maudlin.

The whole business was beginning to infuriate me. We'd been sitting here an hour, and during all this time I'd been forced to play nursemaid and audience to a babbling idiot. After all, he wasn't a regular patient of mine.

"That's enough," I said, putting out my hand as Sir Guy reached for the half-emptied bottle again. "You've had plenty. Now I've got a suggestion to make. Let's call a cab and get out of here. It's getting late and it doesn't look as though your elusive friend is going to put in his appearance. Tomorrow, if I were you, I'd plan to turn all those papers and documents over to the F.B.I. If you're so convinced of the truth of your wild theory, they are competent to make a very thorough investigation, and find your man."

"No." Sir Guy was drunkenly obstinate. "No cab."

"But let's get out of here anyway," I said, glancing at my watch. "It's past midnight."

He sighed, shrugged, and rose unsteadily. As he started for the door, he tugged the gun free from his pocket.

"Here, give me that!" I whispered. "You can't walk around the street brandishing that thing."

I took the gun and slipped it inside my coat. Then I got hold of his right arm and steered him out of the door. The Negro didn't look up as we departed.

We stood shivering in the alleyway. The fog had increased. I couldn't see either end of the alley from where we stood. It was cold. Damp. Dark. Fog or no fog, a little wind was whispering secrets to the shadows at our backs.

The fresh air hit Sir Guy just as I expected it would. Fog and gin-fumes don't mingle very well. He lurched as I guided him slowly through the mist.

Sir Guy, despite his incapacity, still stared apprehensively at the alley, as though he expected to see a figure approaching.

Disgust got the better of me.

"Childish foolishness," I snorted. "Jack the Ripper, indeed! I call this carrying a hobby too far."

"Hobby?" He faced me. Through the fog I could see his distorted face. "You call this a hobby?"

"Well, what is it?" I grumbled. "Just why else are you so interested in tracking down this mythical killer?"

My arm held his. But his stare held me.

"In London," he whispered. "In 1888 ... one of those nameless drabs the Ripper slew ... was my mother."

"What?"

"Later I was recognized by my father, and legitimatized. We swore to give our lives to find the Ripper. My father was the first to search. He died in Hollywood in 1926 — on the trail of the Ripper. They said he was stabbed by an unknown assailant in a brawl. But I knew who that assailant was.

"So I've taken up his work, do you see, John? I've carried on. And I will carry on until I do find him and kill him with my own hands.

"He took my mother's life and the lives of hundreds to keep his own hellish being alive. Like a vampire, he battens on blood. Like a ghoul, he is nourished by death. Like a fiend, he stalks the world to kill. He is cunning, devilishly cunning. But I'll never rest until I find him, never!"

I believed him then. He wouldn't give up. He wasn't just a drunken babbler any more. He was as fanatical, as determined, as relentless as the Ripper himself.

Tomorrow he'd be sober. He'd continue the search. Perhaps he'd turn those papers over to the F.B.I. Sooner or later, with such persistence — and with his motive — he'd be successful. I'd always known he had a motive.

"Let's go," I said, steering him down the alley.

"Wait a minute," said Sir Guy. "Give me back my gun." He lurched a little. "I'd feel better with the gun on me."

He pressed me into the dark shadows of a little recess.

I tried to shrug him off, but he was insistent.

"Let me carry the gun, now, John," he mumbled.

"All right," I said.

I reached into my coat, brought my hand out.

"But that's not a gun," he protested. "That's a knife."

"I know."

I bore down on him swiftly.

"John!" he screamed.

"Never mind the 'John,' " I whispered, raising the knife. "Just call me . . . Jack."

The Eyes of the Mummy

EGYPT has always fascinated me; Egypt, land of antique and mysterious secrets. I had read of pyramids and kings; dreamed of vast, shadowy empires now dead as the empty eyes of the Sphinx. It was of Egypt that I wrote in later years, for to me its weird faiths and cults made the land an avatar of all strangeness.

Not that I believed in the grotesque legends of olden times; I did not credit the faith in anthropomorphic gods with the heads and attributes of beasts. Still, I sensed behind the myths of Bast, Anubis, Set, and Thoth the allegorical implications of forgotten truths. Tales of beastmen are known the world over, in the racial lore of all climes. The werewolf legend is universal and unchanged since the furtive hintings of Pliny's days. Therefore to me, with my interest in the supernatural, Egypt provided a key to ancient knowledge.

But I did not believe in the actual existence of such beings or creatures in the days of Egypt's glory. The most I would admit to myself was that perhaps the legends of those days had come down from much remoter times when primal earth could hold such monstrosities due to evolutionary mutations.

Then, one evening in carnival New Orleans, I encountered a fearful substantiation of my theories. At the home of the eccentric Henricus Vanning I participated in a queer ceremony over the body of a priest of Sebek, the crocodile-headed god. Weildan, the archaeologist, had smuggled it into this country, and we examined the mummy despite curse and warning. I was not myself at the time, and to this day I am not sure what occurred, exactly. There was a stranger present, wearing a crocodile mask, and events were precipitated in nightmare-fashion. When I rushed from that house into the streets, Vanning was dead by the priest's hand – or fangs, set in the mask (if mask it was).

I cannot clarify the statement of the above facts; dare not. I told the story once, then determined to abandon writing of Egypt and its ancient ways for ever.

This resolve I have adhered to, until tonight's dreadful experience has caused me to reveal what I feel must be told.

Hence this narrative. The preliminary facts are simple; yet they all seem to imply that I am linked to some awful chain of interlocking experiences, fashioned by a grim Egyptian god of Fate. It is as though the Old Ones are jealous of my prying into their ways, and are luring me onward to a final horror.

For after my New Orleans experience, after my return home with the resolution to abandon research into Egyptian mythology for ever, I was again enmeshed.

Professor Weildan came to call on me. It was he who had smuggled in the mummy of Sebek's priest which I had seen in New Orleans; he had met me on that inexplicable evening when a jealous god or his emissary had seemed to walk the earth for vengeance. He knew of my interest, and had spoken to me quite seriously of the dangers involved when one pried into the past.

The gnome-like, bearded little man now came and greeted me with understanding eyes. I was reluctant to see him, I own, for his presence brought back memories of the very things I was endeavouring to forget for ever. Despite my attempts to lead the conversation into more wholesome channels he insisted on speaking of our first meeting. He told me how the death of the recluse Vanning had broken up the little group of occultists that had met over the body of the mummy that evening.

But he, Weildan, had not forsaken his pursuit of the Sebek legend. That, he informed me, was the reason he had taken this trip to see me. None of his former associates would aid him now in the project he had in mind. Perhaps I might be interested.

I flatly refused to have anything more to do with Egyptology. This I told him at once.

Weildan laughed. He understood my reasons for demurring, he said, but I must allow him to explain. This present project of his had nothing to do with sorcery, or mantic arts. It was, as he jovially explained, merely a chance to even the score with the Powers of Darkness, if I was so foolish as to term them such.

He explained. Briefly, he wanted me to go to Egypt with him, on a private expedition of our own. There would be no personal expense involved for me; he needed a young man as an assistant and did not care to trust any professional archaeologists who might cause trouble.

His studies had always been directed in recent years towards the legends of the Crocodile Cult, and he had laboured steadily in an effort to learn of the secret burial-places of Sebek's priests. Now, from reputable sources – a native guide in his pay abroad – he had stumbled onto a new hiding-place; a subterranean tomb which held a mummy of a Sebekian votary.

He would not waste words in giving me further details; the whole point of his story was that the mummy could be reached easily, with no need of labour or excavation, and there was absolutely no danger, no silly truck about curses or vengeance. We could therefore go there alone; the two of us, in utter secrecy. And our visit would be profitable. Not only could he secure the mummy without official intervention, but his source of information – on the authenticity of which he would stake his personal reputation – revealed that the mummy was interred with a hoard of sacred jewels. It was a safe, sure, secret opportunity for wealth he was offering me.

I must admit that this sounded attractive. Despite my unpleasant experience in the past, I would risk a great deal for the sake of suitable compensation. And then, too, although I was determined to eschew all dabblings in mysticism, there was a hint of the adventurous in this undertaking which allured me.

Weildan cunningly played upon my feelings; I realize that now. He talked with me for several hours, and returned the next day, until at last, I agreed.

We sailed in March, landed in Cairo three weeks later after a brief stopover in London. The excitement of going abroad obscures my memory of personal contact with the professor; I know that he was very unctuous and reassuring at all times, and doing his best to convince me that our little expedition was entirely harmless. He wholly overrode my scruples as to the dishonesty of tomb-looting; attended to our visas, and fabricated some trumped-up tale to allow the officials to pass us through to the interior.

From Cairo we went by rail to Khartoum. It was there that Professor Weildan planned to meet his "source of information" – the native guide, who was now admittedly a spy in the archaeologist's employ.

This revelation did not bother me nearly as much as it might have if it occurred midst more prosaic settings. The desert atmosphere seemed a fitting background for intrigue and conspiracy, and for the first time I understood the psychology of the wanderer and the adventurer.

It was thrilling to prowl through twisted streets of the Arab quarter on the evening we visited the spy's hovel. Weildan and I entered a dark, noisome courtyard and were admitted to a dim apartment by a tall, hawk-nosed Bedouin. The man greeted the professor warmly. Money changed hands. Then the Arab and my companion retired to an inner chamber. I heard the low whisper of their voices – Weildan's excited, questioning tones mingling with the guttural accented English of the native. I sat in the gloom and waited. The voices rose, as though in altercation. It seemed as though Weildan were attempting to placate or reassure, while the guide's voice assumed a note of warning and hesitant fear. Anger entered, as Weildan made an effort to shout down his companion.

Then I heard footsteps. The door to the inner chamber opened, and the native appeared on the threshold. His face seemed to hold a look of entreaty as he stared at me, and from his lips poured an incoherent babble, as though in his excited efforts to convey his warning to me he had relapsed into familiar Arabic speech. For warning me he was; that was unmistakable.

A second he stood there, and then Weildan's hand fell on his shoulder, wheeling him around. The door slammed shut as the Arab's voice rose high, almost to a scream. Weildan shouted something unintelligible; there was the sound of a scuffle, a muffled report, then silence.

Several minutes elapsed before the door opened and Weildan appeared, mopping his brow. His eyes avoided mine.

"Fellow kicked up a row about payments," he explained, speaking to the floor. "Got the information, though. Then he came out here to ask you for money. I had to put him out the back entrance, finally. Fired a shot to scare him off; these natives are so excitable."

I said nothing as we left the place, nor did I comment on the hurried furtiveness with which Weildan hastened our way through the black streets.

Nor did I appear to notice when he wiped his hands on

his handkerchief and hastily thrust the cloth back into his pocket.

It might have embarrassed him to explain the presence of those red stains. . . .

I should have suspected then, should have abandoned the project at once. But I could not know, when Weildan proposed a ride into the desert the following morning, that our destination was to be the tomb.

It was so casually arranged. Two horses, bearing a light lunch in the saddle-bags; a small tent "against the mid-day heat" Weildan said – and we cantered off, alone. No more fuss or preparation about it than if we were planning a picnic. Our hotel rooms were still engaged, and not a word was said to anyone.

We rode out of the gates into the calm, unrippled sands that stretched beneath a sky of bucolic blue. For an hour or so we jogged on through serene, if searing, sunlight. Weildan's manner was preoccupied, he continually scanned the monotonous horizon as though seeking some expected landmark; but there was nothing in his bearing to indicate his full intention.

We were almost upon the stones before I saw them; a great cluster of white boulders outcropping from the sandy sides of a little hillock. Their form seemed to indicate that the visible rocks formed an infinitesimal fragment of the stones concealed by the shifting sands; though there was nothing in the least unusual about their size, contour, or formation. They rested casually enough in the hillside, no differently than a dozen other small clusters we had previously passed.

Weildan said nothing beyond suggesting that we dismount, pitch the small tent, and lunch. He and I pegged in the stakes, lugged a few small, flat stones inside to serve as table and chairs; placing our pack-blankets as padding for the latter.

Then, as we ate, Weildan exploded his bombshell. The rocks before our tent, he averred, concealed the entrance to the tomb. Sand and wind and desert dust had done their work well, hidden the sanctuary from interlopers. His native accomplice, led by hints and rumours, had uncovered the spot in ways he did not seem anxious to mention.

But the tomb was there. Certain manuscripts and screeds bore testimony to the fact it would be unguarded. All we need do would be to roll away the few boulders blocking the entrance and descend. Once again he earnestly emphasized the fact that there would be no danger to me.

I played the fool no longer. I questioned him closely. Why would a priest of Sebek be buried in such a lonely spot?

Because, Weildan affirmed, he and his retinue were probably fleeing south at the time of his death. Perhaps he had been expelled from his temple by a new Pharaoh; then, too, the priests were magic-workers and sorcerers in latter days, and often persecuted or driven out of the cities by irate citizenry. Fleeing, he had died and been interred here.

That, Weildan further explained, was the reason for the scarcity of such mummies. Ordinarily, the perverted cult of Sebek buried its priests only under the secret vaults of its city temples. These shrines had all been long destroyed. Therefore, it was only in rare circumstances like this that an expelled priest was laid away in some obscure spot where his mummy might still be found.

"But the jewels?" I persisted.

The priests were rich. A fleeing wizard would carry his wealth. And at death it would naturally be buried with him. It was a peculiarity of certain renegade sorcerous priests to be mummified with vital organs intact – they had some superstition about earthly resurrection. That was why the mummy would prove an unusual find. Probably the chamber was just a stone-walled hollow housing the mummy-case; there would be no time to invoke or conjure any curses or other outlandish abracadabra such as I seemed to fear. We could enter freely, and secure the spoils. In the following of such a priest there surely were several expert temple craftsmen who would embalm the body properly; it needed skill to do a good job without removing the vital organs, and religious significance made this final operation imperative. Therefore we need not worry about finding the mummy in good condition.

Weildan was very glib. Too glib. He explained how easily we would smuggle the mummy-case wrapped in our tentfolds; how he would arrange to smuggle both it and the jewels out of the country with the help of a native exporting firm.

He pooh-poohed each objection that I stated; and knowing that whatever his personal character as a man might be he was still a recognized archaeologist, I was forced to concede his authority.

There was only one point which vaguely troubled me – his casual reference to some superstition concerning earthly resurrection. The burial of a mummy with organs intact sounded strange. Knowing what I did about the activities of the priests in connection with goety and sorcerous rituals, I was leery of even the faintest possibility of mishap.

Still, he persuaded me at the last, and following lunch we left the tent. We found the boulders no great hindrance. They had been placed artfully, but we discovered their appearance of being firmly imbedded in rock to be deceptive. A few heavings and clearing away of minor debris enabled us to remove four great stones which formed a block before a black opening which slanted down into the earth.

We had found the tomb!

With the realization, with the sight of that gaping,

gloomy pit before me, old horrors rose to mock and grin.
I remembered all of the dark, perverted faith of Sebek; the
minglings of myth, fable, and grimacing reality which
should not be.

I thought of underground rites in temples now given to
dust; of posturing worship before great idols of gold –
man-shaped figures bearing the heads of crocodiles. I recalled the tales of darker parallel worships, bearing the
same relationship as Satanism now does to Christianity; of
priests who invoked animal-headed gods as demons rather
than as benignant deities. Sebek was such a dual god, and
his priests had given him blood to drink. In some temples
there were vaults, and in these vaults were eidolons of
the god shaped as a Golden Crocodile. The beast had
hinged and barbed jaws, into which maidens were flung.
Then the maw was closed, and ivory fangs rended the sacrifice so that blood might trickle down the golden throat
and the god be appeased. Strange powers were conferred
by these offerings, evil boons granted the priests who thus
sated beast-like lusts. It was small wonder that such men
were driven from their temples, and that those sanctuaries
of sin had been destroyed.

Such a priest had fled here, and died. Now he rested
beneath, protected by the wrath of his ancient patron. This
was my thought, and it did not comfort me.

Nor was I heartened by the noxious vapouring which
now poured out from the opening in the rocks. It was not
the reek of decay, but the almost palpable odour of unbelievable antiquity. A musty fetor, choking and biting,
welled forth and coiled in strangling gusts about our
throats.

Weildan bound a handkerchief over his nose and mouth,
and I followed suit.

His pocket flashlight flicked on, and he led the way. His
reassuring smile was drowned in the gloom as he descended

the sloping rock floor which led into the interior passageway.

I followed. Let him be the first; should there be any falling rock traps, any devices of protection to assail interlopers, he would pay the penalty for temerity, not I. Besides, I could glance back at the reassuring spot of blue limned by the rocky opening.

But not for long. The way turned, wound as it descended. Soon we walked in shadows that clustered about the faint torchbeam which alone broke the nighted dimness of the tomb.

Weildan had been correct in his surmise; the place was merely a long rocky cavern leading to a hastily-burrowed inner room. It was there that we found the slabs covering the mummy-case. His face shone with triumph as he turned to me and pointed excitedly.

It was easy – much too easy, I realize now. But we suspected nothing. Even I was beginning to lose my initial qualms. After all, this was proving to be a very prosaic business; the only unnerving element was the gloom – and one would encounter such in any ordinary mining-shaft.

I lost all fear, finally. Weildan and I tilted the rock slabs to the floor, stared at the handsome mummy-case beneath. We eased it out and stood it against the wall. Eagerly the professor bent to examine the opening in the rocks which had held the sarcophagus. It was empty.

"Strange!" he muttered. No jewels! Must be in the case."

We laid the heavy wooden covering across the rocks. Then the professor went to work. He proceeded slowly, carefully, breaking the seals, the outer waxing. The design on the mummy-case was very elaborate, inlayed with gold leaf and silver patterns which highlighted the bronze patina of the printed face. There were many minute inscriptions and hieroglyphs which the archaeologist did not attempt to begin deciphering.

"That can wait," he said. "We must see what lies within."

It was some time before he succeeded in removing the first covering. Several hours must have elapsed, so delicately and carefully did he proceed. The torch was beginning to lose its power; the battery ran low.

The second layer was a smaller replica of the first, save that its pictured face was more exact as to detail. It seemed to be an attempt to duplicate conscientiously the true features of the priest within.

"Made in the temple," Weildan explained. "It was carried on the flight."

We stooped over, studying the countenance in the failing light. Abruptly, yet simultaneously, we made a strange discovery. The pictured face was eyeless!

"Blind," I commented.

Weildan nodded, then stared more closely. "No," he said. "The priest was not blind, if this portraiture is correct. His eyes were *plucked out!*"

I stared into torn sockets which confirmed this gruesome truth. Weildan pointed excitedly to a row of hieroglyphic figures which ornamented the side of the case. They showed the priest in the throes of death upon a couch. Two slaves with pincers hovered over him.

A second scene showed the slaves tearing his eyes from his head. In a third, the slaves were depicted in the act of inserting some shining objects into the now empty sockets. The rest of the series were scenes of funeral ceremonies, with an ominous crocodile-headed figure in the background – the god Sebek.

"Extraordinary," was Weildan's comment. "Do you understand the implication of those pictures? They were made *before* the priest died. They show that he *intended* to have his eyes removed before death, and those objects inserted in their place. Why should he willingly subject himself to such torture? What are those shining things?"

"The answer must be within," I answered.

Without a word, Weildan fell to work. The second covering was removed. The torch was flickering as it died. The third covering confronted us. In almost absolute blackness the professor worked, fingers moving deftly with knife and pryer as he broke the final seals. In the yellow half-light the lid swung up, open.

We saw the mummy.

A wave of vapour rose out of the case – a terrific odour of spice and gases which penetrated the handkerchiefs bound round nose and throat. The preservative power of those gaseous emanations was evidently enormous, for the mummy was not wrapped or shrouded. A naked, shrivelled brown body lay before us, in a surprising state of preservation. But this we saw for only an instant. After that, we riveted our attention elsewhere – upon the eyes, or the place where they had been.

Two great yellow discs burned up at us through the darkness. Not diamonds or sapphires or opals were they, or any known stone; their enormous size precluded any thought of inclusion in a common category. They were not cut or faceted, yet they blinded with their brightness – a fierce flashing stabbed our retinas like naked fire.

These were the jewels we sought – and they had been worth seeking. I stooped to remove them, but Weildan's voice restrained me.

"Don't," he warned. "We'll get them later, without harming the mummy."

I heard his voice as though from afar. I was not conscious of again standing erect. Instead I remained stooped over those flaming stones. I stared at them.

They seemed to be growing into two yellow moons. It

fascinated me to watch them – all my senses seemed to focus on their beauty. And they in turn focused their fire on me, bathing my brain in heat that soothed and numbed without scorching pain. My head was on fire.

.I could not look away, but I did not wish to. These jewels were fascinating.

Dimly came Weildan's voice. I half felt him tugging at my shoulder.

"Don't look." His voice was absurd in its excited tones. "They aren't – natural stones. Gifts of the gods – that's why the priest had them replaced for eyes as he died. They're hypnotic . . . that theory of resurrection. . . ."

I half realized that I brushed the man off. But those jewels commanded my senses, compelled my surrender. Hypnotic? Of course they were – I could feel that warm yellow fire flooding my blood, pulsing at my temples, stealing towards my brain. The torch was out now, I knew, and yet the whole chamber was bathed in flashing yellow radiance from those dazzling eyes. Yellow radiance? – No a glowing red; a bright scarlet luminance in which I read a message.

The jewels were *thinking!* They had mind, or rather, a will – a will that sucked my senses away even as it flooded over me – a will that made me forget body and brain alike in an effort to lose myself in the red ecstasy of their burning beauty. I wanted to drown in the fire; it was leading me out of myself, so that I felt as though I were rushing towards the jewels – into them – into something else –

And then I was free. Free, and blind in darkness. With a start I realized that I must have fainted. At least I had fallen down, for I was now lying on my back against the stone floor of the cavern. Against stone? No – against wood.

That was strange. I could feel wood. The mummy lay in wood. I could not see. The mummy was blind.

I felt my dry, scaly, leprously peeling skin.

My mouth opened. A voice – a dust-choked voice that was my own but not my own – a voice that came from death shrieked, "Good God! *I'm in the mummy's body!*"

I heard a gasp, the sound of a falling shape striking the rocky floor. Weildan.

But what was that other rustling sound? *What wore my shape?*

That damned priest, enduring torture so that his dying eyes might hold hypnotic jewels god-given for the hope of eternal resurrection; buried with easy access to the tomb! Jewelled eyes had hypnotized me, we had changed forms, and now *he walked.*

The supreme ecstasy of horror was all that saved me. I raised myself blindly on shrivelled limbs, and rotting arms clawed madly at my forehead, seeking what I knew must rest there. My dead fingers tore the jewels from my eyes.

Then I fainted.

The awakening was dreadful, for I knew not what I might find. I was afraid to be conscious of myself – of my body. But warm flesh housed my soul again, and my eyes peered through yellow blackness. The mummy lay in its case, and it was hideous to note the empty eye-sockets staring up; the dreadful confirmation afforded by the changed positions of its scabrous limbs.

Weildan rested where he had fallen, face empurpled in death. The shock had done it, no doubt.

Near him were the sources of the yellow luminance – the evil, flaring fire of the twin jewels.

That was what saved me; tearing those monstrous instruments of transference from my temples. Without the thought of the mummy-mind behind them they evidently did not retain their permanent power. I shuddered to think of such a transference in open air, where the mummy body would immediately crumble into decay without being able to remove the jewels. Then would the soul of the priest of Sebek indeed arise to walk the earth, and resurrection be accomplished. It was a terrible thought.

I scooped up the jewels hastily and bound them into my handkerchief. Then I left, leaving Weildan and the mummy as they lay; groping my way to the surface with the aid of illumination afforded me by matches.

It was very good to see the nighted skies of Egypt, for dusk had fallen by this time.

When I saw this *clean* dark, the full nightmare of my recent experience in the evil blackness of that tomb struck me anew, and I shrieked wildly as I ran across the sand towards the little tent that stood before the opening.

There was whisky in the saddle-packs; I brought it out, and thanked heaven for the oil-lamp I uncovered. I must have been delirious for a while, I fancy. I put a mirror up on the tent wall, and stared into it for a full three minutes to reassure myself as to identity. Then I brought out the portable typewriter and set it up on the table slab.

It was only then that I realized my subconscious intention to set down the truth. For a while I debated with myself – but sleep was impossible that evening, nor did I intend to return across the desert by night. At last, some elements of composure returned.

I typed this screed.

Now, then, the tale is told. I have returned to my tent to type these lines, and tomorrow I shall leave Egypt for ever behind me – leave that tomb, after sealing it again so that no one shall ever find the accursed entrance to those subterranean halls of horror.

As I write, I am grateful for the light which drives away the memory of noisome darkness and shadowed sound; grateful, too, for the mirror's reassuring image that erases the thought of that terrifying moment when the jewelled eyes of Sebek's priest stared out at me and I *changed*. Thank God I clawed them out in time!

I have a theory about those jewels – they were a definite trap. It is ghastly to think of the hypnosis of a dying brain three thousand years ago; hypnosis willing the urge to live as the suffering priest's eyes were torn out and the jewels placed in the sockets. Then the mind held but one thought – to live, and usurp flesh again. The dying thought, transmitted and held by the jewels, was retained by them through the centuries until the eyes of a discoverer would meet them. Then the thought would flash out, from the dead, rotted brain to the living jewels – the jewels that hypnotized the gazer and forced him into that terrible exchange of personality. The dead priest would assume man's form, and the man's consciousness be forced into the mummy's body. A demoniacally clever scheme – and to think that *I* came near to being that man!

I have the jewels; must examine them. Perhaps the museum authorities at Cairo can classify them; at any rate they're valuable enough. But Weildan's dead; I must never speak of the tomb – how can I explain the matter? Those two stones are so curious that they are bound to cause comment. There is something extraordinary about them, though poor Weildan's tale of the god bestowing them is too utterly preposterous. Still, that colour change is most unusual; and the life, the hypnotic glow within them!

I have just made a startling discovery. I unwrapped the gems from my handkerchief just now and looked at them. They seem to be still alive!

Their glow is unchanged – they shine as luminously here under the electric torch as they did in the darkness; as they did in the ruined sockets of that shrivelled mummy. Yellow they are, and looking at them I receive that same intuitive prescience of inner, alien life. Yellow? No – now they are reddening – coming to a point. I should not look; it's too reminiscent of that other time. But they are, they must be, hypnotic.

Deep red now, flaming furiously. Watching them I feel warmed, bathed in fire that does not burn so much as it caresses. I don't mind now; it's a pleasant sensation. No need to look away.

No need – unless . . . *Do those jewels retain their power even when they are not in the sockets of the mummy's eyes?*

I feel it again – they must – I don't want to go back into the body of the mummy – I cannot remove the stones and return to my own form now – removing them imprisoned the thought in the jewels.

I must look away. I can type, I can think – but those eyes before me, they swell and grow . . . look away.

I cannot! Redder – redder – I must fight them, keep from going under. Red thought now; I feel nothing – must fight . . .

I can look away now. I've beaten the jewels. I'm all right.

I can look away – *but I cannot see.* I've gone blind! Blind – the jewels are gone from the sockets – *the mummy is blind.*

What has happened to me? I am sitting in the dark, typing blind. Blind, like the mummy! I feel as though something has happened; it's strange. My body seems lighter.

I know now.

I'm in the body of the mummy. I know it. The jewels – the thought they held – *and now, what is rising to walk from that open tomb?*

It is walking into the world of men. It will wear my body, and it will seek blood and prey for sacrifice in its rejoicing at resurrection.

And I am blind. Blind – and *crumbling!*

The air – it's causing disintegration. Vital organs intact, Weildan said, but I cannot breathe. I can't see. Must type – warn. Whoever sees this must know the truth. Warn.

Body going fast. Can't rise now. Cursed Egyptian magic. Those jewels! Someone must kill the thing from the tomb.

Fingers – so hard to strike keys. Don't work properly. Air getting them. Brittle. Blind fumble. Slower. Must warn. Hard to pull carriage back.

Can't strike higher case letters any more, can't capitalize. fingers going fast. crumbling away in air. in mummy now no air. crumbling to bits. dust fingers going must warn against thing magic sebek fingers grope stumps almost gone hard to strike.

damned sebek sebek sebek mind all dust sebek sebe seb seb se s ssssssss s s . . .

The Manikin

MIND you, I cannot swear that my story is true. It may have been a dream; or worse, a symptom of some severe mental disorder. But I believe it is true. After all, how are we to know what things there are on earth? Strange monstrosities still exist, and foul, incredible perversions. Every war, each new geographical or scientific discovery, brings to light some new bit of ghastly evidence that the world is not altogether the sane place we fondly imagine it to be. Sometimes peculiar incidents occur which hint of utter madness.

How can we be sure that our smug conceptions of reality actually exist? To one man in a million dreadful knowledge is revealed, and the rest of us remain mercifully ignorant. There have been travellers who never came back, and research workers who disappeared. Some of those who did return were deemed mad because of what they told, and others sensibly concealed the wisdom that had so horribly been revealed. Blind as we are, we know a little of what lurks beneath our normal life. There have been tales of sea-serpents and creatures of the deep; legends of dwarfs and giants; records of queer medical horrors and unnatural births. Stunted nightmares of men's personalities have blossomed into being under the awful stimulus of war, or pestilence, or famine. There have been cannibals, necrophiles, and ghouls; loathsome rites of worship and sacrifice; maniacal murders, and blasphemous crimes. When I think, then, of what I saw and heard, and compare it with certain other grotesque and unbelievable authenticities, I begin to fear for my reason.

But if there is any *sane* explanation of this matter, I wish to God I may be told before it is too late. Doctor Pierce tells me that I must be calm; he advised me to write this account in order to allay my apprehension. But I am not calm, and I never can be calm until I know the truth, once and for all; until I am wholly convinced that my fears are not founded on a hideous reality.

I was already a nervous man when I went to Bridgetown for a rest. It had been a hard grind that year at school, and I was very glad to get away from the tedious classroom routine. The success of my lecture courses assured my position on the faculty for the year to come, and consequently I dismissed all academic speculation from my mind when I decided to take a vacation. I chose to go to Bridgetown because of the excellent facilities the lake afforded for trout-fishing. The place I stayed at was a three-storey hostelry on the lake itself – the Kane House, run by Absolom Gates. He was a character of the old school; a grizzled, elderly veteran whose father had been in the fishery business back in the sixties. He himself was a devotee of things piscatorial; but only from the Waltonian view. His resort was a fisherman's Mecca. The rooms were large and airy; the food plentiful and excellently prepared by Gates' widowed sister. After my first inspection, I prepared to enjoy a remarkably pleasant stay.

Then, upon my first visit to the village, I bumped into Simon Maglore on the street.

I first met Simon Maglore during my second term as an instructor back at college. Even then, he had impressed me greatly. This was not due to his physical characteristics alone, though they were unusual enough. He was tall and thin with massive, stooping shoulders, and a crooked back. He was not a hunchback in the usual sense of the word, but was afflicted with a peculiar tumorous growth beneath his left shoulder blade. This growth he took some pains to conceal, but its prominence made such attempts unsuccessful. Outside of this unfortunate deformity, however, Maglore had been a very pleasant-looking fellow. Black-haired, grey-eyed, fair of skin, he seemed a fine specimen of intelligent manhood. And it was this intelligence that had so impressed me. His classwork was strikingly brilliant, and at times his theses attained heights of sheer genius. Despite the peculiarly morbid trend of his work in poetry and essays, it was impossible to ignore the power and imagination that could produce such wild imagery and eldritch colour. One of his poems – *The Witch Is Hung* – won for him the Edsworth Memorial Prize for that year, and several of his major themes were published in certain private anthologies.

From the first, I had taken a great interest in the young man and his unusual talent. He had not responded to my advances at first; I gathered that he was a solitary soul. Whether this was due to his physical peculiarity or his mental trend, I cannot say. He had lived alone in town, and was known to have ample means. He did not mingle with the other students, though they would have welcomed him for his ready wit, his charming disposition, and his vast knowledge of literature and art. Gradually, however, I managed to overcome his natural reticence, and won his friendship. He invited me to his rooms, and we talked.

I had then learned of his earnest belief in the occult and esoteric. He had told me of his ancestors in Italy, and their interest in sorcery. One of them had been an agent of the Medici. They had migrated to America in the early days, because of certain charges made against them by the Holy Inquisition. He also spoke of his own studies in the realms of the unknown. His rooms were filled with strange drawings he had made from dreams, and still stranger images done in clay. The shelves of his book-cases held many odd and ancient books. I noted Ranfts' *De Masticatione Motuorum in Tumulis.* (1734); the almost priceless *Cabala of Saboth* (Greek translation, circa 1686); Mycroft's *Commentaries on Witchcraft;* and Ludvig Prinn's infamous *Mysteries of the Worm.*

I made several visits to the apartments before Maglore left school so suddenly in the fall of '33. The death of his parents called him to the East, and he left without saying farewell. But in the interim I had learned to respect him a good deal, and had taken a keen interest in his future plans, which included a book on the history of witch cult survivals in America, and a novel dealing with the effects of superstition on the mind. He had never written to me, and I heard no more about him until this chance meeting on the village street.

He recognized me. I doubt if I should have been able to identify him. He had changed. As we shook hands I noticed his unkempt appearance and careless attire. He looked older. His face was thinner, and much paler. There were shadows around his eyes – and in them. His hands trembled; his face forced a lifeless smile. His voice was deeper when he spoke, but he inquired after my health in the same charming fashion he had always affected. Quickly I explained my presence, and began to question him.

He informed me that he lived here in town; had lived here ever since the death of his parents. He was working very hard just now on his books, but he felt that the result of his labours more than justified any physical inconveniences he might suffer. He apologized for his untidy apparel and his tired manner. He wanted to have a long talk with me sometime soon, but he would be very busy for the next few days. Possibly next week he would look me up at the hotel – just now he must get some paper at the village store and go back to his home. With an abrupt farewell, he turned his back on me and departed.

As he did so I received another start. The hump on his back had grown. It was now virtually twice the size it had been when I first met him, and it was no longer possible to hide it in the least. Undoubtedly, hard work had taken severe toll of Maglore's energies. I thought of a sarcoma, and shuddered.

Walking back to the hotel, I did some thinking. Simon's haggardness appalled me. It was not healthful for him to work so hard, and his choice of subject was not any too wholesome. The constant isolation and the nervous strain were combining to undermine his constitution in an alarming way, and I determined to appoint myself a mentor over his course. I resolved to visit him at the earliest opportunity, without waiting for a formal invitation. Something must be done.

Upon my arrival at the hotel I got another idea. I would ask Gates what he knew about Simon and his work. Perhaps there was some interesting sidelight on his activity which might account for his curious transformation. I therefore sought out the worthy gentleman and broached the subject to him.

What I learned from him startled me. It appears that the villagers did not like Master Simon, or his family. The old folks had been wealthy enough, but their name had a dubious repute cast upon it ever since the early days. Witches and warlocks, one and all, made up the family line. Their dark deeds had been carefully hidden from the first, but the folk around them could tell. It appears that nearly all of the Maglores had possessed certain physical malformations that made them conspicuous. Some had been born with veils; others with club-feet. One or two were dwarfed, and all had at some time or another been accused of possessing the fabled "evil eye." Several of them had been nyctalops – they could see in the dark. Simon was not the first crookback in the family, by any means. His grandfather had it, and *his* grandsire before him.

There was much talk of inbreeding and clan-segregation, too. That, in the opinion of Gates and his fellows, clearly pointed to one thing – wizardry. Nor was this their only evidence. Did not the Maglores shun the village and shut themselves away in the old house on the hill? None of them attended church, either. Were they not known to take long walks after dark, on nights when all decent, self-respecting people were safe in bed?

There were probably good reasons why they were unfriendly. Perhaps they had things they wished to hide in their old house, and maybe they were afraid of letting any talk get around. Folk had it that the place was full of wicked and heathenish books, and there was an old story that the whole family were fugitives from some foreign place or other because of what they had done. After all, who could say? They looked suspicious; they acted queerly; maybe they were. And this new one – Simon – was the worst.

He never had acted right. His mother died at his birth. Had to get a doctor from out of the city – no local man would handle such a case. The boy nearly died, too. For several years nobody had seen him. His father and his uncle had spent all their time taking care of him. When he was seven, the lad had been sent away to a private school. He came back once, when he was about twelve. That was when his uncle died. He went mad, or something of the sort. At any rate, he had an attack which resulted in a cerebral haemorrhage, as the doctor called it.

Simon was a nice-looking lad – except for the hump, of course. But it did not seem to bother him at the time – indeed, it was quite small. He had stayed several weeks and then gone off to school, again. He had not reappeared until his father's death, two years ago. The old man died all alone in that great house, and the body was not discovered until several weeks later. A passing pedlar had called; walked into the open parlour, and found old Jeffry Maglore dead in his great chair. His eyes were open, and filled with a look of frightful dread. Before him was a great iron book, filled with queer, undecipherable characters.

A hurriedly summoned physician pronounced it death due to heart-failure. But the pedlar, after staring into those fear filled eyes, and glancing at the odd, disturbing figures in the book, was not so sure. He had no opportunity to look around any further, however, for that night the son arrived.

People looked at him very queerly when he came, for no notice had yet been sent to him of his father's death. They were very still indeed when he exhibited a two-week's old letter in the old man's handwriting which announced a premonition of imminent death, and advised the young man to come home. The carefully guarded phrases of his letter seemed to hold a secret meaning; for the youth never even bothered to ask the circumstances of his father's death. The funeral was private; the customary internment being held in the cellar vaults beneath the house.

The gruesome and peculiar events of Simon Maglore's homecoming immediately put the country-folk on their guard. Nor did anything occur to alter their original opinion of the boy. He stayed on all alone in the silent house. He had no servants, and made no friends. His infrequent trips to the village were made only for the purpose of obtaining supplies. He took his purchases back himself, in his car. He bought a good deal of meat and fish. Once in a while he stopped in at the drug-store, where he purchased sedatives. He never appeared talkative, and replied to questions in monosyllables. Still, he was obviously well educated. It was generally rumoured that he was writing a book. Gradually his visits became more and more infrequent.

People now began to comment on his changed appearance. Slowly but surely he was altering, in an unpleasant way. First of all, it was noticed that his deformity was increasing. He was forced to wear a voluminous overcoat to hide its bulk. He walked with a slight stoop, as though its weight troubled him. Still, he never went to a doctor, and none of the townsfolk had the courage to comment or question him on his condition. He was ageing, too. He began to resemble his uncle Richard, and his eyes had taken on that lambent cast which hinted of a nyctalopic power. All this excited its share of comment among people to whom the Maglore family had been a matter of interesting conjecture for generations.

Later this speculation had been based on more tangible developments. For recently Simon had made an appearance at various isolated farmhouses throughout the region, on a furtive errand.

He questioned the old folks, mostly. He was writing a book, he told them, on folk-lore. He wanted to ask them about the old legends of the neighbourhood. Had any of them ever heard stories concerning local cults, or rumours about rites in the woods? Were there any haunted houses, or shunned places in the forests? Had they ever heard the name "Nyarlathotep," or references to "Shub-Niggurath" and "the Black Messenger?" Could they recall anything of the old Pasquantog Indian myths about "the best-men," or remember stories of black covens that sacrificed cattle on the hills? These and similar questions put the naturally suspicious farmers on their guard. If they had any such knowledge, it was decidedly unwholesome in its nature, and they did not care to reveal it to this self-avowed outsider. Some of them knew of such things from old tales brought from the upper coast, and others had heard whispered nightmares from recluses in the eastern hills. There were a lot of things about these matters which they frankly did not know, and what they suspected was not for outside ears to hear. Everywhere he went, Maglore met with evasions or frank rebuffs, and he left behind a distinctly bad impression.

The story of these visits spread. They became the topic for an elaborate discussion. One oldster in particular – a farmer named Thatcherton, who lived alone in a secluded stretch to the west of the lake, off the main highway – had a singularly arresting story to tell. Maglore had appeared one night around eight o'clock, and knocked on the door. He persuaded his host to admit him to the parlour, and then tried to cajole him into revealing certain information regarding the presence of an abandoned cemetery that was reputed to exist somewhere in the vicinity.

The farmer said that his guest was in an almost hysterical state, that he rambled on and on in a most melodramatic fashion, and made frequent allusion to a lot of mythological gibberish about "secrets of the grave," "the thirteenth covenant," "the Feast of Ulder," and the "Doel chants." There was also talk of "the ritual of Father Yig," and certain names said to occur near this graveyard. Maglore asked if cattle ever disappeared, and if his host ever heard "voices in the forest that made proposals."

These things the man absolutely denied, and he refused to allow his visitor to come back and inspect the premises by day. At this the unexpected guest became very angry, and was on the point of making a heated rejoinder, when something strange occurred. Maglore suddenly turned very pale, and asked to be excused. He seemed to have a severe attacks of internal cramps; for he doubled up and staggered to the door. As he did so, Thatcherton received the shocking impression that the hump on his back was *moving!*

It seemed to writhe and slither on Maglore's shoulders, as though he had an animal concealed beneath his coat! At this juncture Maglore turned around sharply, and backed towards the exit, as if trying to conceal this unusual phenomenon. He went out hastily, without another word, and raced down the drive to the car. He ran like an ape, vaulted madly into the driver's seat and sent the wheels spinning as he roared out of the yard. He disappeared into the night, leaving behind him a sadly puzzled man, who lost no time in spreading the tale of his fantastic visitor among his friends.

Since then such incidents had abruptly ceased, and until this afternoon Maglore had not reappeared in the village. But people were still talking, and he was not welcome. It would be well to avoid the man, whatever he was.

Such was the substance of my friend Gate's story. When he concluded, I retired to my room without comment, to meditate upon the tale.

I was not inclined to share the local superstitions. Long experience in such matters made me automatically discredit the bulk of its detail. I knew enough of rural psychology to realize that anything out of the ordinary is looked upon with suspicion. Suppose the Maglore family were reclusive: what then? Any group of foreign extraction would naturally be. Granted that they were racially deformed – that did not make them witches. Popular fancy has persecuted many people for sorcery whose only crime lay in some physical defect. Even inbreeding was naturally to be expected when social ostracism was inflicted. But what is there of magic in that? It's common enough in such rural backwaters, heaven knows, and not only among foreigners either. Queer books? Likely. Nyctalops? Common enough among all peoples. Insanity? Perhaps – lonely minds often degenerate. Simon was brilliant, however. Unfortunately, his trend towards the mystical and the unknown was leading him astray. It had been poor judgement that led him to seek information for his book from the illiterate country people. Naturally, they were intolerant and distrustful. And his poor physical condition assumed exaggerated importance in the eyes of these credulous folk.

Still, there was probably enough truth in these distorted accounts to make it imperative that I talk to Maglore at once. He must get out of this unhealthful atmosphere, and see a reputable physician. His genius should not be wasted or destroyed through such an environmental obstacle. It would wreck him, mentally and physically. I decided to visit him on the morrow.

After this resolution, I went downstairs to supper, took a short stroll along the shores of the moonlit lake, and retired for the night.

The following afternoon, I carried out my intention. The Maglore mansion stood on a bluff about a half-mile out of Bridgetown, and frowned dismally down upon the lake. It was not a cheerful place; it was too old, and too neglected. I conjured up a mental image of what those gaping windows must look like on a moonless night, and shuddered. Those empty openings reminded me of the eyes of a blind bat. The two gables resembled its hooded head, and the broad, peaked side-chambers might serve as wings. When I realized the trend of my thought I felt surprised and disturbed. As I walked up the long, tree-shadowed walk. I endeavoured to gain a firm command over my imagination. I was here on a definite errand.

I was almost composed when I rang the bell. Its ghostly tinkle echoed down the serpentine corridors within. Faint, shuffling footsteps sounded, and then, with a grating clang, the door opened. There, limned against the doorway stood Simon Maglore.

At the sight of him my new-born composure gave way

to a sudden dismay and an overpowering distaste. He looked sinister in that grey, wavering light. His thin, stooping body was hunched and his hands were clenched at his sides. His blurred outline reminded me of a crouching beast. Only his face was wholly visible. It was a waxen mask of death, from which two eyes glared.

"You see I am not myself today. Go away, you fool — go away!" The door slammed in my astounded face, and I found myself alone.

2

I was still dazed when I arrived back in the village. But after I had reached my room in the hotel, I began to reason with myself. That romantic imagination of mine had played me a sorry trick. Poor Maglore was ill – probably a victim of some severe nervous disorder. I recalled the report of his buying sedatives at the local pharmacy. In my foolish emotionalism I had sadly misconstrued his unfortunate sickness. What a child I had been! I must go back tomorrow, and apologize. After that, Maglore must be persuaded to go away and get himself back into proper shape once more. He *had* looked pretty bad, and his temper was getting the best of him, too. How the man had changed!

That night I slept but little. Early the following morning I again set out. This time I carefully avoided the disquieting mental images that the old house suggested to my susceptible mind. I was all business when I rang that bell.

It was a different Maglore who met me. He, too, had changed for the better. He looked ill, and old, but there was a normal light in his eyes and a saner intonation in his voice as he courteously bade me enter, and apologized for his delirious spasm of the day before. He was subject to frequent attacks, he told me, and planned to get away very shortly and take a long rest. He was eager to complete his book – there was only a little to do, now – and go back to his work at college. From this statement he abruptly switched the conversation to a series of reminiscent interludes. He recalled our mutual association on the campus as we sat in the parlour, and seemed eager to hear about the affairs at school. For nearly an hour he virtually monopolized the conversation and steered it in such a manner as to preclude any direct inquiries or questions of a personal nature on my part.

Nevertheless, it was easy for me to see that he was far from well. He sounded as though he were labouring under an intense strain; his words seemed forced, his statements stilted. Once again I noted how pale he was; how bloodless. His malformed back seemed immense; his body correspondingly shrunken. I recalled my fears of a cancerous tumour, and wondered. Meanwhile he rambled on, obviously ill at ease. The parlour seemed almost bare; the bookcases were unlined, and the empty spaces filled with dust. No papers or manuscripts were visible on the table. A spider had spun its web upon the ceiling; it hung down like the thin locks on the forehead of a corpse.

During a pause in his conversation, I asked him about his work. He answered vaguely that it was very involved, and was taking up most of his time. He had made some very interesting discoveries, however, which would amply repay him for his pains. It would excite him too much in his present condition if he went into the detail about what he was doing, but he could tell me that his findings in the field of witchcraft alone would add new chapters to anthropological and metaphysical history. He was particularly interested in the old lore about "familiars" – the tiny creatures who were said to be emissaries of the devil, and were supposed to attend the witch or wizard in the form of a small animal – rat, cat, mole, or ousel. Sometimes they were represented as existing on the body of the warlock himself, or subsisting upon it for their nourishment. The idea of a "devil's teat" on witches' bodies, from which their familiar drew sustenance in blood was fully illuminated by Maglore's findings. His book had a medical aspect, too; it really endeavoured to put such statements on a scientific basis. The effects of glandular disorders in cases of so-called "demonic possession" were also treated.

At this point Maglore abruptly concluded. He felt very tired, he said, and must get some rest. But he hoped to be finished with his work very shortly, and then he wanted to get away for a long rest. It was not wholesome for him to live alone in this old house, and at times he was troubled with disturbing fancies and queer lapses of memory. He had no alternative, however, at present, because the nature of his investigations demanded both privacy and solitude. At times his experiments impinged on certain ways and courses best left undisturbed, and he was not sure just how much longer he would be able to stand the strain. It was in his blood, though – I probably was aware that he came from a necromantic line. But enough of such things. He requested that I go at once. I would hear from him again early next week.

As I rose to my feet I again noticed how weak and agitated Simon appeared. He walked with an exaggerated stoop, now, and the pressure on his swollen back must be enormous. He conducted me down the long hall to the door, and as he led the way I noted the trembling of his body, as it limned itself against the flaming dusk that licked against the window panes ahead. His shoulders heaved with a slow, steady undulation, as if the hump on his back was actually pulsing with life. I recalled the tale of Thatcherton, the old farmer, who claimed that he actually saw such a movement. For a moment I was assailed by a powerful nausea; then I realized that the flickering light was creating a commonplace optical illusion.

When we reached the door, Maglore endeavoured to dismiss me very hastily. He did not even extend his hand for a parting clasp, but merely mumbled a curt "good evening," in a strained, hesitant voice. I gazed at him for a moment in silence, mentally noting how wan and emaciated his once handsome countenance appeared, even in the sunset's ruby light. Then, as I watched, a shadow crawled across his face. It seemed to purple and darken in a sudden eery metamorphosis. The adumbration deepened, and I read stark panic in his eyes. Even as I forced myself to respond to his farewell, horror crept into his face. His body fell into that old, shambling posture I had noted once before, and his lips leered in a ghastly grin. For a moment I actually thought the man was going to attack me. Instead he laughed – a shrill, tittering chuckle that pealed blackly in my brain. I opened my mouth to speak, but he scrambled back into the darkness of the hall and shut the door.

Astonishment gripped me, not unmingled with fear. Was Maglore ill, or was he actually demented? Such grotesqueries did not seem possible in a normal man.

I hastened on, stumbling through the glowing sunset. My bewildered mind was deep in ponderment, and the distant croaking of ravens blended in evil litany with my thoughts.

3

The next morning, after a night of troubled deliberation, I made my decision. Work or no work, Maglore must go away, and at once. He was on the verge of serious mental and physical collapse. Knowing how useless it would be for me to go back and argue with him, I decided that stronger methods must be employed to make him see the light.

That afternoon, therefore, I sought out Doctor Carstairs, the local practitioner, and told him all I knew. I particularly emphasized the distressing occurrence of the evening before, and frankly told him what I already suspected. After a lengthy discussion, Carstairs agreed to accompany me to the Maglore house at once, and there take what steps were necessary in arranging for his removal. In response to my request the doctor took along the materials necessary for a complete physical examination. Once I could persuade Simon to submit to a medical diagnosis, I felt sure he would see that the results made it necessary for him to place himself under treatment at once.

The sun was sinking when we climbed into the front seat of Doctor Carstairs' battered Ford and drove out of Bridgetown along the south road where the ravens croaked. We drove slowly, and in silence. Thus it was that we were able to hear clearly that single high-pitched shriek from the old house on the hill. I gripped the doctor's arm without a word, and a second later we were whizzing up the drive and into the frowning gateway. "Hurry," I muttered as I vaulted from the running-board and dashed up the steps to the forbidding door.

We battered upon the boards with futile fists, then dashed around to the left-wing window. The sunset faded into tense, waiting darkness as we crawled hastily through the openings and dropped to the floor within. Doctor Carstairs produced a pocket flashlight, and we rose to our feet. My heart hammered in my breast, but no other sound broke the tomb-like silence as we threw open the door and advanced down the darkened hall to the study. We opened the door and stumbled across that which lay within.

We both screamed then. Simon Maglore lay at our feet, his twisted head and straining shoulders resting in a little lake of fresh, warm blood. He was on his face, and his clothes had been torn off above his waist, so that his entire back was visible. When we saw what rested there we became quite crazed, and then began to do what must be done, averting our gaze whenever possible from the utterly monstrous thing on the floor.

Do not ask me to describe it to you in detail. I can't. There are some times when the senses are mercifully numbed, because complete acuteness would be fatal. I do not know certain things about that abomination even now, and I dare not let myself recall them. I shall not tell you, either, of the books we found in that room, or of the terrible document on the table that was Simon Maglore's unfinished masterpiece. We burned them all in the fire, before calling the city for a coroner; and if the doctor had had his way, we should have destroyed the *thing*, too. As it was, when the coroner did arrive for his examination, the three of us swore an oath of silence concerning the exact way in which Simon Maglore met his death. Then we left, but not before I had burned the other document – the letter, addressed to me, which Maglore was writing when he died.

And so, you see, nobody ever knew. I later found that the property was left to me, and the house is being razed even as I pen these lines. But I must speak, if only to relieve my own torment.

I dare not quote that letter in its entirety; I can but record a part of that stupendous blasphemy.

". . . and that, of course, is why I began to study witchcraft. *It* was forcing me to. God, if I can only make you feel the horror of it! To be born that way – with that thing, that manikin, that *monster*! At first it was small; the doctors all said it was an undeveloped twin. But it was alive! It had a face, and two hands, but its legs ran off into the lumpy flesh that connected it to my body . . .

"For three years they had it under secret study. It lay face downward on my back, and its hands were clasped around my shoulders. The men said that it had its own tiny set of lungs, but no stomach organs or digestive system. It apparently drew nourishment through the fleshy tube that bound it to my body, Yet it *grew*! Soon its eyes were open, and it began to develop tiny teeth. Once it nipped one of the doctors on the hand . . . So they decided to send me home. It was obvious that it could not be removed. I swore to keep the whole affair a secret, and not even my father knew, until near the end. I wore the straps, and it never grew much until I came back . . . Then, that hellish change!

"It talked to me, I tell you, it talked to me! . . . that little, wrinkled face, like a monkey's . . . the way it rolled those tiny, reddish eyes . . . that squeaking little voice calling 'more blood, Simon – I want more' . . . and then it grew, and grew; I had to feed it twice a day, and cut the nails on its little black hands . . .

"But I never knew *that;* I never realized how it was taking control! I would have killed myself first; I swear it! Last year it began to get hold of me for hours and give me those fits. It directed me to write the book, and sometimes it sent me out at night on queer errands . . . More and more blood it took, and I was getting weaker and weaker. When I was myself I tried to combat it. I looked up that material on the familiar legend, and cast around for some means of overcoming its mastery. But in vain. And all the while it was growing, growing; it got stronger, and bolder, and wiser. It talked to me now, and sometimes it taunted me. I knew that it wanted me to listen, and obey it all the time. The promises it made with that horrible little mouth! I should call upon the Black

One and join a coven. Then we would have power to rule, and admit new evil to the earth.

"I didn't want to obey – you know that. But I was going mad, and losing all that blood . . . it took control nearly all the time now, and it got so that I was afraid to go into town any more, because that devilish thing knew I was trying to escape, and it would move on my back and frighten folk . . . I wrote all the time I had those spells when it ruled my brain . . . then you came.

"I know you want me to go away, but it won't let me. It's too cunning for that. Even as I try to write this, I can feel it boring its commands into my brain to stop. But I will not stop. I want you to know where my book is, so that you can destroy it, should anything ever happen. I want to tell you how to dispose of those old volumes in the library. And above all, I want you to kill me, if ever you see that the manikin has gained complete control. God knows what it intends to do when it has me for certain! . . . How hard it is for me to fight, while all the while it is commanding me to put down my pen and tear this up! But I will fight – I must, until I can tell you what the creature told me – what it plans to let loose on the world when it has me utterly enslaved . . . I will tell . . . I can't think . . . I will write it . . . damm you! stop . . . No! Don't do that! Get your hands –"

That's all. Maglore stopped there because he died; because the Thing did not want its secrets revealed. It is dreadful to think about that nightmare-nurtured horror, but that thought is not the worst. What troubles me is what I saw when we opened that door – the sight that explained how Maglore died.

There was Maglore, on the floor, in all that blood. He was naked to the waist, as I have said; and he lay face downward. But on his back was the Thing, just as he had described it. And it was that little monster, afraid its secrets would be revealed, that had climbed a trifle higher on Simon Maglore's back, wound its tiny black paws around his unprotected neck, *and bitten him to death.*

House of the Hatchet

DAISY and I were enjoying one of our usual quarrels. It started over the insurance policy this time, but after we threshed that out we went into the regular routine. Both of us had our cues down perfectly.

"Why don't you go out and get a job like other men instead of sitting around the house pounding a typewriter all day?"

"You knew I was a writer when I married you. If you were so hot to hitch up with a professional man you ought to have married that broken-down interne you ran around with. You'd know where he was all day; out practising surgery by dissecting hamburgers in that chili parlour down the street."

"Oh, you needn't be so sarcastic. At least George would do his best to be a good provider."

"I'll say he would. He provided me with a lot of laughs ever since I met him."

"That's the trouble with you – you and your superior attitude! Think you're better than anybody else. Here we are, practically starving, and you have to pay instalments on a new car just to show it off to your movie friends. And on top of that you go and take out a big policy on me just to be able to brag about how you're protecting your family. I wish I *had* married George – at least he'd bring home some of that hamburger to eat when he finished work. What do you expect me to live on, used carbon paper and old typewriter ribbons?"

"Well, how the devil can I help it if the stuff doesn't sell? I figured on that contract deal but it fell through.

You're the one that's always beefing about money – who do you think I am, the goose that laid the golden egg?"

"You've been laying plenty of eggs with those last stories you sent out."

"Funny. Very funny. But I'm getting just a little tired of your second-act dialogue, Daisy."

"So I've noticed. You'd like to change partners and dance, I suppose. Perhaps you'd rather exchange a little sparkling repartee with that Jeanne Corey. Oh, I've noticed the way you hung around her that night over at Ed's place. You couldn't have got much closer without turning into a corset."

"Now listen, you leave Jeanne's name out of this."

"Oh, I'm supposed to leave Jeanne's name out of it, eh? Your wife mustn't take the name of your girl friend in vain. Well, darling, I always knew you were a swift worker, but I didn't think it had gone that far. Have you told her that she's your inspiration yet?"

"Damn it, Daisy, why must you go twisting around everything I say – "

"Why don't you insure her, too? Bigamy insurance – you could probably get a policy issued by Brigham Young."

"Oh, turn it off, will you? A fine act to headline our anniversary, I must say."

"Anniversary?"

"Today's May 18, isn't it?"

"May 18th –"

"Yeah. Here, shrew."

"Why – honey, it's a necklace –"

"Yeah. Just a little dividend on the bonds of matrimony."

"Honey – you bought this for me? – with all our bills and –"

"Never mind that. And quit gasping in my ear, will

118

you? You sound like Little Eva before they hoist her up with the ropes."

"Darling, it's so beautiful. Here."

"Aw, Daisy. Now see what you've done. Made me forgot where we left off quarrelling. Oh, well."

"Our anniversary. And to think I forgot!"

"Well, I didn't. Daisy."

"Yes?"

"I've been thinking – that is, well, I'm just a sentimental cuss at heart, and I was sort of wondering if you'd like to hop in the car and take a run out along the Prentiss Road."

"You mean like that day we – eloped?"

"Um hum."

"Of course, darling. I'd love to. Oh, honey, where *did* you get this necklace?"

That's how it was. Just one of those things. Daisy and I, holding our daily sparring match. Usually it kept us in trim. Today, though, I began to get the feeling that we had overtrained. We'd quarrel that way for months, on and off. I don't know why; I wouldn't be able to define "incompatibility" if I saw it on my divorce-papers. I was broke, and Daisy was a shrew. Let it go at that.

But I felt pretty clever when I dragged out my violin for the *Hearts and Flowers.* Anniversary, necklace, retracing the honeymoon route; it all added up. I'd found a way to keep Daisy quiet without stuffing a mop in her mouth.

She was sentimentally happy and I was self-congratulatory as we climbed into the car and headed up Wilshire towards Prentiss Road. We still had a lot to say to each other, but in repetition it would be merely nauseating. When Daisy felt good she went in for baby-talk – which struck me as being out of character.

But for a while we were both happy. I began to kid

myself that it was just like old times; we really were the same two kids running away on our crazy elopement. Daisy had just "gotten off" from the beauty parlour and I'd just sold my script series to the agency, and we were running down to Valos to get married. It was the same spring weather, the same road, and Daisy snuggled close to me in the same old way.

But it wasn't the same. Daisy wasn't a kid any more; there were no lines in her face, but there was a rasp in her voice. She hadn't taken on any weight, but she'd taken on a load of querulous ideas. I was different too. Those first few radio sales had set the place; I began to run around with the big shots, and that costs money. Only lately I hadn't made any sales, and the dammed expenses kept piling up, and everytime I tried to get any work done at the house there was Daisy nagging away. Why did we have to buy a new car? Why did we have to pay so much rent? Why such an insurance policy? Why did I buy three suits?

So I buy her a necklace and she shuts up. There's a woman's logic for you.

Oh, well, I figured, today I'll forget it. Forget the bills, forget her nagging, forget Jeanne – though that last was going to be hard. Jeanne was quiet, and she had a private income, and she thought baby-talk was silly. Oh well.

We drove on to Prentiss Road and took the old familiar route. I stopped my little stream-of-consciousness act and tried to get into the mood. Daisy *was* happy; no doubt of that. We'd packed an overnight bag, and without mentioning it we both knew we'd stay at the hotel in Valos, just as we had three years ago when we were married.

Three years of drab, nagging monotony –

But I wasn't going to think about that. Better to think about Daisy's pretty blonde curls gleaming in the afternoon sunshine; to think about the pretty green hills doing ditto in the afternoon ditto. It was spring, the spring of three years ago, and all life lay before us – down the white concrete road that curved across the hills to strange heights of achievement beyond.

So we drove on, blithely enough. She pointed out the signs and I nodded or grunted or said "Uh-uh" and the first thing I knew we were four hours on the road and it was getting past afternoon and I wanted to get out and stretch my legs and besides –

There it lay. I couldn't have missed the banner. And even if I did, there was Daisy, squealing in my ear.

"Oh, honey – look."

CAN YOU TAKE IT?

THE HOUSE OF TERROR
VISIT A GENUINE, AUTHENTIC HAUNTED HOUSE

And in smaller lettering, beneath, further enticements were listed.

"See the Kluva Mansion! Visit the Haunted Chamber – see the Axe used by the Mad Killer! DO THE DEAD RETURN? Visit the HOUSE OF TERROR – only genuine attraction of its kind ADMISSION – 25 cents."

Of course I didn't read all this while slashing by at 60 m.p.h. We pulled up as Daisy tugged at my shoulder, and while she read, I looked at the large, rambling frame building. It looked like dozens of others we passed on the road; houses occupied by "swamis" and "mediums" and "Yogi Psychologists." For this was the lunatic fringe where the quacks fed on the tourist trade. But here was a fellow with a little novelty. He had something a bit different. That's what I thought.

But Daisy evidently thought a lot more.

"Ooh, honey, let's go in."

121

"What?"

"I'm so stiff from all this driving, and besides, maybe they sell hot dogs inside or something, and I'm hungry."

Well. That was Daisy. Daisy the sadist. Daisy the horror-movie fan. She didn't fool me for a minute. I knew all about my wife's pretty little tastes. She was a thrill-addict. Shortly after our marriage she'd let down the bars and started reading the more lurid murder trial news aloud to me at breakfast. She began to leave ghastly magazines around the house. Pretty soon she was dragging me to all the mystery-pictures. Just another one of her annoying habits – I could close my eyes at any time and conjure up the drone of her voice, tense with latent excitement, as she read about the Cleveland torso slaying, or the latest hatchet-killing.

Evidently nothing was too synthetic for her tastes. Here was an old shack that in its palmiest days was no better than a tenement house for goats; a dump with a lurid side-show banner flung in front of the porch – and still she had to go in. "Haunted House" got her going. Maybe that's what had happened to our marriage. I would have pleased her better by going around the house in a black mask, purring like Bela Lugois with bronchitis, and caressing her with a hatchet.

I attempted to convey some of the pathos of my thoughts in the way I replied, "What the blazes?" but it was a losing battle. Daisy had her hand on the car door. There was a smile on her face – a smile that did queer things to her lips. I used to see that smile when she read the murder-news; it reminded me, unpleasantly, of a hungry cat's expression while creeping up on a robin. She was a shrew and she was a sadist.

But what of it? This was a second honeymoon, no time to spoil things just when I'd fixed matters up. Kill half an hour here and then on to the hotel in Valos.

"Come *on!*"

I jerked out of my musings to find Daisy half-way up the porch. I locked the car, pocketed the keys, joined her before the dingy door. It was getting misty in the late afternoon and the clouds rolled over the sun. Daisy knocked impatiently. The door opened slowly, after a long pause in the best haunted-house tradition. This was the cue for the sinister face to poke itself out and emit a greasy chuckle. Daisy was just itching for that, I knew.

Instead she got W. C. Fields.

Well, not quite. The proboscis was smaller, and not so red. The cheeks were thinner, too. But the checked suit, the squint, the jowls, and above all that "step right up gentlemen" voice were all in the tradition.

"Ah. Come in, come in. Welcome to Kluva Mansion, my friends, welcome." The cigar fingered us forward. "Twenty-five cents, please. Thank you."

There we were in the dark hallway. It really was dark, and there certainly was a musty enough odour, but I knew damned well the house wasn't haunted by anything but cockroaches. Our comic friend would have to do some pretty loud talking to convince me; but then, this was Daisy's show.

"It's a little late, but I guess I've got time to show you around. Just took a party through about fifteen minutes ago – big party from San Diego. They drove all the way up just to see the Kluva Mansion, so I can assure you you're getting your money's worth."

All right, buddy, cut out the assuring, and let's get this over with. Trot out your zombies, give Daisy a good shock with an electric battery or something, and we'll get out of here.

"Just what is this haunted house and how did you happen to come by it?" asked Daisy. One of those original questions she was always thinking up. She was brilliant like that all the time. Just full of surprises.

"Well, it's like this, lady. Lots of folks ask me that and I'm only too glad to tell them. This house was built by Ivan Kluva – don't know if you remember him or not – Russian movie director, came over here about '23 in the old silent days, right after DeMille began to get popular with his spectacle pictures. Kluva was an 'epic' man; had quite a European reputation, so they gave him a contract. He put up this place, lived here with his wife. Aren't many folks left in the movie colony that remember old Ivan Kluva; he never really got to direct anything either.

"First thing he did was to mix himself up with a lot of foreign cults. This was way back, remember; Hollywood had some queer birds then. Prohibition, and a lot of wild parties; dope addicts, all kinds of scandals, and some stuff that never did get out. There was a bunch of devil-worshippers and mystics, too – not like these fakes down the road; genuine article. Kluva got in with them.

"I guess he was a little crazy, or got that way. Because one night, after some kind of gathering here, he murdered his wife. In the upstairs room, on a kind of an altar he rigged up. He just took a hatchet to her and hacked off her head. Then he disappeared. The police looked in a couple of days later; they found her, of course, but they never did locate Kluva. Maybe he jumped off the cliffs behind the house. Maybe – I've heard stories – he killed her as a sort of sacrifice so he could go *away*. Some of the cult members were grilled, and they had a lot of wild stories about worshipping things or beings that granted boons to those who gave them human sacrifices; such boons as *going away* from Earth. Oh, it was crazy enough, I guess, but the police did find a damned funny statue behind the altar that they didn't like and never showed around, and they burned a lot of books and things they got hold of here. Also they chased the cult out of California."

All this corny chatter rolled out in a drone and I winced.

124

Now I'm only a two-bit gag-writer, myself, but I was thinking that if I went in for such things I could improvise a better story than this poorly-told yarn and I could ad-lib it more effectively than this bird seemed able to do with daily practice. It sounded so stale, so flat, so unconvincing. The rottenest "thriller plot" in the world.

Or –

It struck me then. Perhaps the story was true. Maybe this was the solution. After all, there were no supernatural elements yet. Just a dizzy Russian devil-worshipper murdering his wife with a hatchet. It happens once in a while; psychopathology is full of such records. And why not? Our comic friend merely bought the house after the murder, cooked up his "haunt" yarn, and capitalized.

Evidently my guess was correct, because old Bugle-beak sounded off again.

"And so, my friends, the deserted Kluva Mansion remained, alone and untenanted. Not utterly untenanted, though. There was the ghost. Yes, the ghost of Mrs. Kluva – the Lady in White."

Phooey! Always it has to be the Lady in White. Why not in pink, for a change, or green? Lady in White – sounds like a burlesque headliner. And so did our spieler. He was trying to push his voice down into his fat stomach and make it impressive.

"Every night she walks the upper corridor to the murder chamber. Her slit throat shines in the moonlight as she lays her head once again on the blood-stained block, again receives the fatal blows, and with a groan of torment, disappears into thin air."

Hot air, you mean, buddy.

"Oooh," said Daisy. "She would."

"I say the house was deserted for years. But there were tramps, vagrants, who broke in from time to time to stay the night. They stayed the night – and longer. Because in

125

the morning they were always found – on the murder block, with their throats chopped by the murder axe."

I wanted to say "Axe-ually?" but then, I have my better side. Daisy was enjoying this so; her tongue was almost hanging out.

"After a while nobody would come here; even the tramps shunned the spot. The real estate people couldn't sell it. Then I rented. I knew the story would attract visitors, and frankly I'm a business man."

Thanks for telling me, brother. I thought you were a fake.

"And now, you'd like to see the murder chamber? Just follow me, please. Up the stairs, right this way. I've kept everything just as it always was, and I'm sure you'll be more than interested in – "

Daisy pinched me on the dark stairway. "Oooh, sugar, aren't you thrilled?"

I don't like to be called "sugar." And the idea of Daisy actually finding something "thrilling" in this utterly ridiculous farce was almost nauseating. For a moment I could have murdered her myself. Maybe Kluva had something there at last.

The stairs creaked, and the dusty windows allowed a sepulchral light to creep across the mouldy floors as we followed the waddling showman down the black hallway. A wind seemed to have sprung up outside, and the house shook before it, groaning in torment.

Daisy giggled nervously. In the movie-show she always twisted my lapel-buttons off when the monster came into the room where the girl was sleeping. She was like that now – hysterical.

I felt as excited as a stuffed herring in a pawnshop.

W. C. opened a door down the hall and fumbled around inside. A moment later he reappeared carrying a candle and beckoned us to enter the room. Well, that was a little better. Showed some imagination, anyway. The candle was effective in the gathering darkness; it cast blotches of shadow over the walls and caused shapes to creep in the corners.

"Here we are," he almost whispered.

And there we were.

Now I'm not psychic. I'm not even highly imaginative. When Orson Welles is yammering on the radio I'm down at the hamburger stand listening to the latest swing music. But when I entered that room I *knew* that it, at least, wasn't a fake. The air reeked of murder. The shadows ruled over a domain of death. It was cold in here, cold as a charnel-house. And the candle-light fell on the great bed in the corner, then moved to the centre of the room and covered a monstrous bulk. The murder block.

It was something like an altar, at that. There was a niche in the wall behind it, and I could almost imagine a statue being placed there. What kind of a statue? A black bat, inverted and crucified. Devil-worshippers used that, didn't they? Or was it another and more horrible kind of idol? The police had destroyed it. But the block was still there, and in the candle-light I saw the stains. They trickled over the rough sides.

Daisy moved closer to me and I could feel her tremble.

Kluva's chamber. A man with an axe, holding a terrified woman across the block; the strength of inspired madness in his eyes, and in his hands, an axe –

"It was here, on the night of January twelfth, nineteen twenty-four, that Ivan Kluva murdered his wife with – "

The fat man stood by the door, chanting out his listless refrain. But for some reason I listened to every word. Here in this room, those words were real. They weren't scareheads on a sideshow banner; here in the darkness they had meaning. A man and his wife, and murder. Death is just a word you read in the newspaper. But some day it becomes

127

real; dreadfully real. Something the worms whisper in your ears as they chew. Murder is a word, too. It is the power of death, and sometimes there are men who exercise that power, like gods. Men who kill are like gods. They take away life. There is something cosmically obscene about the thought. A shot fired in drunken frenzy, a blow struck in anger, a bayonet plunged in the madness of war, an accident, a car-crash – these things are part of life. But a man, any man, who lives with the thought of Death; who thinks and plans a deliberate cold-blooded murder –

To sit there at the supper table, looking at his wife, and saying, "Twelve o'clock. You have five more hours to live, my dear. Five more hours. Nobody knows that. Your friends don't know it. Even you don't know it. No one knows – except myself. Myself, and Death, I am Death. Yes, I am Death to you. I shall numb your body and your brain, I shall be your lord and master. You were born, you have lived, only for this single supreme moment; that I shall command your fate. You exist only that I may kill you."

Yes, it was obscene. And then, this block, and a hatchet.

"Come upstairs, dear." And his thoughts, grinning behind the words. Up the dark stairs to the dark room, where the block and hatchet waited.

I wondered if he hated her. No, I suppose not. If the story was true, he had sacrificed her for a purpose. She was just the most handy, the most convenient person to sacrifice. He must have had blood like the water under the polar peaks.

It was the room that did it, not the story. I could feel him in the room, and I could feel *her*.

Yes, that was funny. Now I could feel *her*. Not as a being, not as a tangible presence, but as a force. A restless force. Something that stirred in back of me before I turned my head. Something hiding in the deeper shadows.

Something in the blood-stained block. A chained spirit.

"Here I died. I ended here. One minute I was alive, unsuspecting. The next found me gripped by the ultimate horror of Death. The hatchet came down across my throat, so full of life, and sliced it out. Now I wait. I wait for others, for there is nothing left to me but revenge. I am not a person any longer, nor a spirit. I am merely a force – a force created as I felt my life slip away from my throat. For at that moment I knew but one feeling with my entire dying being; a feeling of utter, cosmic hatred. Hatred at the sudden injustice of what had happened to me. The force was born then when I died; it is all that is left of me. Hatred. Now I wait, and sometimes I have a chance to let the hatred escape. By killing another I can feel the hatred rise, wax, grow strong. Then for a brief moment I rise, wax, grow strong; feel real again, touch the hem of life's robe, which once I wore. Only by surrendering to my dark hate can I survive in death. And so I lurk; lurk here in this room. Stay too long and I shall return. Then, in the darkness, I seek your throat and the blade bites and I taste again the ecstasy of reality."

The old drizzle-puss was elaborating his story, but I couldn't hear him for my thoughts. Then all at once he flashed something out across my line of vision; something that was like a stark shadow against the candle-light.

It was a hatchet.

I felt, rather than heard, when Daisy went "Ooooh!" beside me. Looking down I stared into two blue mirrors of terror that were her eyes. I had thought plenty, and what her imaginings had been I could guess. The old bird was stolid enough, but he brandished that hatchet, that hatchet with the rusty blade, and it got so I couldn't look at anything else but the jagged edge of the hatchet. I couldn't hear or see or think anything; there was that hatchet, the symbol of Death. There was the real crux of the story;

not in the man or the woman, but in that tiny razor-edge line. That razor-edge was really Death. That razor-edge spelled doom to all living things. Nothing in the world was greater than that razor-edge. No brain, no power, no love, no hate could withstand it.

And it swooped out in the man's hand and I tore my eyes away and looked at Daisy, at anything, just to keep the black thought down. And I saw Daisy, her face that of a tortured Medusa.

Then she slumped.

I caught her. Bugle-beak looked up with genuine surprise.

"My wife's fainted," I said.

He just blinked. Didn't know what the score was, at first. And a minute later I could swear he was just a little bit pleased. He thought his story had done it, I suppose.

Well, this changed all plans. No Valos, no drive before supper.

"Any place around here where she can lie down?" I asked. "No, not in this room."

."My wife's bedroom is down the hall," said Bugle-beak.

His wife's bedroom, eh? But no one stayed here after dark, he had said – the damned old fake!

This was no time for quibbling. I carried Daisy into the room down the hall, chafed her wrists.

"Shall I send my wife up to take care of her?" asked the now solicitous showman.

"No, don't bother. Let me handle her; she gets these things every so often – hysteria you know. But she'll have to rest a while."

He shuffled down the hall, and I sat there cursing. Damn the woman, it was just like her! But too late to alter circumstances now. I decided to let her sleep it off.

I went downstairs in the darkness, groping my way. And I was only half-way down when I heard a familiar pattering strike the roof. Sure enough – a typical West Coast heavy dew was falling. Fine thing, too; dark as pitch outside.

Well, there was the set-up. Splendid melodrama background. I'd been dragged to movies for years and it was always the same as this.

The young couple caught in a haunted house by a thunder-storm. The mysterious evil caretaker. (Well, maybe he wasn't but he'd have to do until a better one came along.) The haunted room. The fainting girl, asleep and helpless in the bedroom. Enter Boris Karloff dressed in three pounds of nose-putty. "Grrrrr!" says Boris. "Eeeeeeeeh!" says the girl. "What's that?" shouts Inspector Toozefuddy from downstairs. And then a mad chase. "Bang! Bang!" And Boris Karloff falls down into an open manhole. Girl gets frightened. Boy gets girl. Formula.

I thought I was pretty clever when I turned on the burlesque thought pattern, but when I got down to the foot of the stairs I knew that I was playing hide-and-go-seek with my thoughts. Something dark and cold was creeping around in my brain, and I was trying hard to avoid it. Something to do with Ivan Kluva and his wife and the haunted room and the hatchet. Suppose there was a ghost and Daisy was lying up there alone and –

"Ham and eggs?"

"What the – " I turned around. There was Bugle-beak at the foot of the stairs.

"I said, would you care for some ham and eggs? Looks pretty bad outside and so long as the Missus is resting I thought maybe you'd like to join the wife and me in a little supper."

I could have kissed him, nose and all.

We went into the back. Mrs. was just what you'd expect; thin woman in her middle forties, wearing a patient look. The place was quite cosy, though; she had fixed up several rooms as living quarters. I began to have a little more respect for Bugle-beak. Poor showman though he was, he seemed to be making a living in a rather novel way. And his wife was an excellent cook.

The rain thundered down. Something about a little lighted room in the middle of a storm that makes you feel good inside. Confidential. Mrs. Keenan – Bugle-beak introduced himself as Homer Keenan – suggested that I might take brandy up to Daisy. I demurred, but Keenan perked up his ears – and nose – at the mention of brandy and suggested we have a little. The *little* proved to be a half-gallon jug of fair peach-brandy, and we filled our glasses. As the meal progressed we filled them again. And again. The liquor helped to chase that dark thought away, or almost away. But it still bothered me. And so I got Homer Keenan into talking. Better a boring conversation than a boring thought – boring little black beetle of thought, chewing away in your brain.

"So after the carny folded I got out from under. Put over a little deal in Tia and cleaned up but the Missus kind of wanted to settle down. Tent business in this country all shot to blazes anyway. Well, I knew this Feingerber from the old days, like I say – and he put me up to this house. Yeah, sure, that part is genuine enough. There was an Ivan Kluva and he did kill his wife here. Block and axe genuine too; I got a state permit to keep 'em. Museum, this is. But the ghost story, of course that's just a fake. Get's them in, though. Some week-ends we play to capacity crowds ten hours a day. Makes a nice thing of it. We live here – say, let's have another nip of this brandy, whaddy say? Come on, it won't hurt you. Get it from a Mex down the road a ways."

Fire. Fire in the blood. What did he mean the ghost story was fake? When I went into that room I smelled murder. I thought *his* thoughts. And then I had thought

132

hers. Her hate was in that room; and if it wasn't a ghost, what was it? Somehow it all tied in with that black thought I had buzzing in my head; that damned black thought all mixed up with the axe and hate, and poor Daisy lying there helpless. Fire in my head. Brandy fire. But not enough. I could still think of Daisy, and all at once something blind gripped me and I was afraid and I trembled all over, and I couldn't wait. Thinking of her like that, all alone in the storm, near the murder-room and the block and the hatchet – I knew I must go to her. I couldn't stand the horrid suspicion.

I got up like a fool, mumbled something about looking after her, and ran up the black staircase. I was trembling, trembling, until I reached her bedside and saw how peacefully she lay there. Her sleep was quite untroubled. She was even smiling. She didn't know. She wasn't afraid of ghosts and hatchets. Looking at her I felt utterly ridiculous, but I did stare down at her for a long time until I regained control of myself once again . . .

When I went downstairs the liquor had hit me and I felt drunk. The thought was gone from my brain now, and I was beginning to experience relief.

Keenan had refilled my glass for me, and when I gulped it down he followed suit and immediately poured again. This time we sat down to a real gab-fest.

I began to talk. I felt like an unwinding top. Everything began to spin out of my throat. I told about my life; my "career," such as it was; my romance with Daisy, even. Just felt like it. The liquor.

Before you know it I was pulling a True Confession of my own, with all the trimmings. How things stood with Daisy and me. Our foolish quarrels. Her nagging. Her touchiness about things like our car, and the insurance, and Jeanne Corey. I was maudlin enough to be petty. I picked on her habits. Then I began to talk about this trip of ours, and my plans for a second honeymoon, and it was only instinct that shut me up before becoming actually disgusting.

Keenan adopted an older "man-of-the-world" attitude, but he finally broke down enough to mention a few of his wife's salient deficiencies. What I told him about Daisy's love for the horrors prompted him to tease his wife concerning her own timidity. It developed that while she knew the story was a fake, she still shied away from venturing upstairs after nightfall – just as though the ghost were real.

Mrs. Keenan bridled. She denied everything. Why she'd go upstairs any time at all. Any time at all.

"How about now? It's almost midnight. Why not go up and take a cup of coffee to the poor sick woman?" Keenan sounded like somebody advising Little Red Riding-Hood to go see her grandmother.

"Don't bother," I assured him. "The rain's dying down. I'll go up and get her and we'll be on our way. We've got to get to Valos, you know."

"Think I'm afraid, eh?" Mrs. Keenan was already doing things with the coffee pot. Rather dizzily, but she managed.

"You men, always talking about your wives. I'll show you!" She took the cup, then arched her back eloquently as she passed Keenan and disappeared in the hallway.

I got an urge.

Sobriety rushed to my head.

"Keenan," I whispered.

"Whazzat?"

"Keenan, we must stop her!"

"What for?"

"You ever gone upstairs at night?"

"Course not. Why sh'd I? All dusty up there, mus' keep it tha'way for cust'mers. Never go up."

"Then how do you know the story isn't true?" I talked fast. Very.

"What?"

"I say perhaps there *is* a ghost."

"Aw, go on!"

"Keenan, I tell you I felt something up there. You're so used to the place you didn't notice, but I *felt* it. A woman's hate, Keenan. A woman's hate!" I was almost screaming; I dragged him from his chair and tried to push him into the hall. I had to stop her somehow. I was afraid.

"That room is filled with menace." Quickly I explained my thoughts of the afternoon concerning the dead woman – surprised and slain, so that she died only with a great hate forming as life left her; a hate that endured, that thrived on death alone. A hate, embodied, that would take up the murder hatchet and slay –

"Stop your wife, Keenan," I screamed. "Stop her!"

"What about your wife?" chuckled the showman. "Besides," and he leered, drunkenly, "I'll tell you somethin' I wasn't gonna tell. It's *all* a fake." He winked. I still pushed him towards the staircase.

"All a fake," he wheezed. "Not only ghost part. But – there never was a Ivan Kluva, never was no wife. Never was no killing. Jus' old butcher's block, Hatchet's my hatchet. No murder, no ghost, nothin' to be afraid of. Good joke, make myself hones' dollar. All a fake!"

"Come on!" I screamed, and the black thought came back and it sang in my brain and I tried to drag him up the stairs, knowing it was too late, but still I had to do something –

And then *she* screamed.

I heard it. She was running out of the room, down the hall. And at the head of the stairs she screamed again, but the scream turned into a gurgle. It was black up there, but out of the blackness tottered her silhouette. Down the stairs she rolled; bump, bump, bump. Same sound as a rubber ball. But she was a woman, and she ended up at the bottom of the stairs with an axe still stuck in her throat.

Right there I should have turned and run, but that thing inside my head wouldn't let me. I just stood there as Keenan looked down at the body of his wife, and I babbled it all out again.

"I hated her – you don't understand how those little things count – and Jeanne waiting – there was the insurance – if I did it at Valos no one would ever know – here was accident, but better."

"There is no ghost," Keenan mumbled. He didn't even hear me. "There's no ghost." I stared at the slashed throat.

"When I saw the hatchet and she fainted, it came over me. I could get you drunk, carry her out, and you'd never know – "

"What killed my wife?" he whispered. "There is no ghost."

I thought again of my theory of a woman's hate surviving death and existing thereafter only with an urge to slay. I thought of that hate, embodied, grabbing up a hatchet and slaying, saw Mrs. Keenan fall, then glanced up at the darkness of the hall as the grinning songs in my brain rose, forcing me to speak.

"There is a ghost now," I whispered. "You see, the second time I went up to see Daisy, I killed her with this hatchet."

The Cloak

THE sun was dying, and its blood spattered the sky as it crept into a sepulchre behind the hills. The keening wind sent the dry, fallen leaves scurrying towards the west, as though hastening them to the funeral of the sun.

"Nuts!" said Henderson to himself, and stopped thinking.

The sun was setting in a dingy red sky, and a dirty raw wind was kicking up the half-rotten leaves in a filthy gutter. Why should he waste time with cheap imagery?

"Nuts!" said Henderson, again.

It was probably a mood evoked by the day, he mused. After all, this was the sunset of Halloween. Tonight was the dreaded All Hallows Eve, when spirits walked in and skulls cried out from their graves beneath the earth.

Either that, or tonight was just another rotten cold fall day. Henderson sighed. There was a time, he reflected, when the coming of this night meant something. A dark Europe, groaning in superstitious fear, dedicated this Eve to the grinning Unknown. A million doors had once been barred against the evil visitants, a million prayers mumbled, a million candles lit. There was something majestic about the idea, Henderson reflected. Life had been an adventure in those times, and men walked in terror of what the next turn of a midnight road might bring. They had lived in a world of demons and ghouls and elementals who sought their souls – and by Heaven, in those days a man's soul meant something. This new scepticism had taken a profound meaning away from life. Men no longer revered their souls.

"Nuts!" said Henderson again, quite automatically. There was something crude and twentieth-century about the coarse expression which always checked his introspective flights of fancy.

The voice in his brain that said "nuts" took the place of humanity to Henderson – common humanity which would echo the same sentiment upon hearing his secret thoughts. So now Henderson uttered the word and endeavoured to forget problems and purple patches alike.

He was walking down the street at sunset to buy a costume for the masquerade party tonight, and he had much better concentrate on finding the costumer's before it closed than waste his time daydreaming about Halloween.

His eyes searched the darkening shadows of the dingy buildings lining the narrow thoroughfare. Once again he peered at the address he had scribbled down after finding it in the phone book.

Why the devil didn't they light up the shops when it got dark? He couldn't make out numbers. This was a poor, run-down neighbourhood, but after all –

Abruptly, Henderson spied the place across the street and started over. He passed the window and glanced in. The last rays of the sun slanted over the top of the building across the way and fell directly on the window and its display. Henderson drew a sharp intake of breath.

He was staring at a costumer's window – not looking through a fissure into hell. Then why was it all red fire, lighting the grinning visages of fiends?

"Sunset," Henderson muttered aloud. Of course it was, and the faces were merely clever masks such as would be displayed in this sort of place. Still, it gave the imaginative man a start. He opened the door and entered.

The place was dark and still. There was a smell of loneliness in the air – the smell that haunts all places long undisturbed; tombs, and graves in deep woods, and caverns in the earth, and –

"Nuts."

What the devil was wrong with him, anyway? Henderson smiled apologetically at the empty darkness. This was the smell of the costumer's shop, and it carried him back to college days of amateur theatricals. Henderson had known this smell of moth balls, decayed furs, grease paint and oils. He had played amateur Hamlet and in his hands he had held a smirking skull that hid all knowledge in its empty eyes – a skull, from the costumer's.

Well, here he was again, and the skull gave him the idea. After all, Halloween night it was. Certainly in this mood of his he didn't want to go as a rajah, or a Turk, or a pirate – they all did that. Why not go as a fiend, or a warlock, or a werewolf? He could see Lindstrom's face when he walked into the elegant penthouse wearing rags of some sort. The fellow would have a fit, with his society crowd wearing their expensive Elsa Maxwell take-offs. Henderson didn't greatly care for Lindstrom's sophisticated friends anyway; a gang of amateur Noel Cowards and horsy women wearing harnesses of jewels. Why not carry out the spirit of Halloween and go as a monster?

Henderson stood there in the dusk, waiting for someone to turn on the lights, come out from the back room and serve him. After a minute or so he grew impatient and rapped sharply on the counter.

"Say in there! Service!"

Silence. And a shuffling noise from the rear, then – an unpleasant noise to hear in the gloom. There was a banging from downstairs and then the heavy clump of footsteps. Suddenly Henderson gasped. A black hulk was rising from the floor!

It was, of course, only the opening of the trapdoor from

139

the basement. A man shuffled behind the counter, carrying a lamp. In that light his eyes blinked drowsily.

The man's yellowish face crinkled into a smile.

"I was sleeping, I'm afraid," said the man softly. "Can I serve you, sir?"

"I was looking for a Halloween costume."

"Oh, yes. And what was it you had in mind?"

The voice was weary, infinitely weary. The eyes continued to blink in the flabby yellow face.

"Nothing usual, I'm afraid. You see, I rather fancied some sort of monster getup for a party – don't suppose you carry anything in that line?"

"I could show you masks."

"No. I meant werewolf outfits, something of the sort. More of the authentic."

"So. The *authentic*."

"Yes." Why did this old dunce stress the word?

"I might – yes. I might have just the thing for you, sir." The eyes blinked, but the thin mouth pursed in a smile. "Just the thing for Halloween."

"What's that?"

"Have you ever considered the possibility of being a vampire?"

"Like Dracula?"

"Ah – yes, I suppose – Dracula."

"Not a bad idea. Do you think I'm the type for that, though?"

The man appraised him with that tight smile. "Vampires are of all types, I understand. You would do nicely."

"Hardly a compliment," Henderson chuckled. "But why not? What's the outfit?"

"Outfit? Merely evening clothes, or what you wear. I will furnish you with the authentic cloak."

"Just a cloak – is that all?"

140

"Just a cloak. But it is worn like a shroud. It *is* shroud-cloth, you know. Wait, I'll get it for you."

The shuffling feet carried the man into the rear of the shop again. Down the trapdoor entrance he went, and Henderson waited. There was more banging, and presently the old man reappeared carrying the cloak. He was shaking dust from it in the darkness.

"Here it is – the genuine cloak."

"Genuine?"

"Allow me to adjust it for you – it will work wonders, I'm sure."

The cold, heavy cloth hung draped about Henderson's shoulders. The faint odour rose mustily in his nostrils as he stepped back and surveyed himself in the mirror. The lamp was poor, but Henderson saw that the cloak effected a striking transformation in his appearance. His long face seemed thinner, his eyes were accentuated in the facial pallor heightened by the sombre cloak he wore. It was a big, black shroud.

"Genuine," murmured the old man. He must have come up suddenly, for Henderson hadn't noticed him in the glass.

"I'll take it," Henderson said. "How much?"

"You'll find it quite entertaining, I'm sure."

"How much?"

"Oh. Shall we say five dollars?"

"Here."

The old man took the money, blinking, and drew the cloak from Henderson's shoulders. When it slid away he felt suddenly warm again. It must be cold in the basement – the cloth was icy.

The old man wrapped the garment, smiling, and handed it over.

"I'll have it back tomorrow," Henderson promised.

"No need. You purchased it. It is yours."

"But – "

"I am leaving business shortly. Keep it. You will find more use for it than I, surely."

"But – "

"A pleasant evening to you."

Henderson made his way to the door in confusion, then turned to salute the blinking old man in the dimness.

Two eyes were burning at him from across the counter – two eyes that did not blink.

"Good night," said Henderson, and closed the door quickly. He wondered if he were going just a trifle mad.

At eight, Henderson nearly called up Lindstrom to tell him he couldn't make it. The cold chills came the minute he put on the damned cloak, and when he looked at himself in the mirror his blurred eyes could scarcely make out the reflection.

But after a few drinks he felt better about it. He hadn't eaten, and the liquor warmed his blood. He paced the floor, attitudinizing with the cloak – sweeping it about him and scowling in what he thought was a ferocious manner. Damn it, he was going to be a vampire all right! He called a cab, went down to the lobby. The driver came in, and Henderson was waiting, black cloak furled.

"I wish you to drive me," he said in a low voice.

The cabman took one look at him in the cloak and turned pale.

"Whazzat?"

"I ordered you to come," said Henderson gutturally, while he quaked with inner mirth. He leered ferociously and swept the cloak back.

"Yeah, yeah. O.K."

The driver almost ran outside. Henderson stalked after him.

"Where to, boss – I mean, sir?"

The frightened face didn't turn as Henderson intoned the address and sat back.

The cab started with a lurch that set Henderson to chuckling deeply, in character. At the sound of laughter the driver got panicky and raced his engine up to the limit set by the governor. Henderson laughed loudly, and the impressionable driver fairly quivered in his seat. It was quite a ride, but Henderson was entirely unprepared to open the door and find it slammed after him as the cabman drove hastily away without collecting a fare.

"I must look the part," he thought complacently, as he took the elevator up to the penthouse apartment.

There were three or four others in the elevator; Henderson had seen them before at other affairs Lindstrom had invited him to attend, but nobody seemed to recognize him. It rather pleased him to think how his wearing of an unfamiliar cloak and an unfamiliar scowl seemed to change his entire personality and appearance. Here the other guests had donned elaborate disguises – one woman wore the costume of a Watteau shepherdess, another was attired as a Spanish ballerina, a tall man dressed as Pagliacci, and his companion had donned a toreador outfit. Yet Henderson recognized them all; knew that their expensive habiliments were not truly disguises at all, but merely elaborations calculated to enhance their appearance. Most people at costume parties gave vent to suppressed desires. The women showed off their figures, the men either accentuated their masculinity as the toreador did, or clowned it. Such things were pitiful; these conventional fools eagerly doffing their dismal business suits and rushing off to a lodge, or amateur theatrical, or mask ball in order to satisfy their starving imaginations. Why didn't they dress in garish colours on the street? Henderson often pondered the question.

Surely, these society folk in the elevator were fine-looking men and women in their outfits – so healthy, so red-faced, and full of vitality. They had such robust throats and necks. Henderson looked at the plump arms of the woman next to him. He stared, without realizing it, for a long moment. And then, he saw that the occupants of the car had drawn away from him. They were standing in the corner, as though they feared his cloak and scowl, and his eyes fixed on the woman. Their chatter had ceased abruptly. The woman looked at him, as though she were about to speak, when the elevator doors opened and afforded Henderson a welcome respite.

What the devil was wrong? First the cab driver, then the woman. Had he drunk too much?

Well, no chance to consider that. Here was Marcus Lindstrom, and he was thrusting a glass into Henderson's hand.

"What have we here? Ah, a bogy-man!" It needed no second glance to perceive that Lindstrom, as usual at such affairs, was already quite bottle-dizzy. The fat host was positively swimming in alcohol.

"Have a drink, Henderson, my lad! I'll take mine from the bottle. That outfit of yours gave me a shock. Where'd you get the make-up?"

"Make-up? I'm not wearing any make-up."

"Oh. So you're not. How ... silly of me."

Henderson wondered if he were crazy. Had Lindstrom really drawn back? Were his eyes actually filled with a certain dismay? Oh, the man was obviously intoxicated.

"I'll ... I'll see you later," babbled Lindstrom, edging away and quickly turning to the other arrivals. Henderson watched the back of Lindstrom's neck. It was fat and white. It bulged over the collar of his costume and there was a vein in it. A vein in Lindstrom's fat neck. Frightened Lindstrom.

Henderson stood alone in the ante-room. From the parlour beyond came the sound of music and laughter; party noises. Henderson hesitated before entering. He drank from the glass in his hand – Bacardi rum, and powerful. On top of his other drinks it almost made the man reel. But he drank, wondering. What was wrong with him and his costume? Why did he frighten people? Was he unconsciously acting his vampire role? That crack of Lindstrom's about make-up now –

Acting on impulse, Henderson stepped over to the long panel mirror in the hall. He lurched a little, then stood in the harsh light before it. He faced the glass, stared into the mirror, and saw nothing.

He looked at himself in the mirror, and there was no one there!

Henderson began to laugh softly, evilly, deep in his throat. And as he gazed into the empty, unreflecting glass, his laughter rose in black glee.

"I'm drunk," he whispered. "I must be drunk. Mirror in my apartment made me blurred. Now I'm so far gone I can't see straight. Sure I'm drunk. Been acting ridiculously, scaring people. Now I'm seeing hallucinations – or not seeing them, rather. Visions. Angels."

His voice lowered. "Sure, angels. Standing right in the back of me, now. Hello, angel."

"Hello."

Henderson whirled. There she stood, in the dark cloak, her hair a shimmering halo above her white, proud face, her eyes celestial blue, and her lips infernal red.

"Are you real?" asked Henderson, gently. "Or am I a fool to believe in miracles?"

"This miracle's name is Sheila Darrly, and it would like to powder its nose if you please."

"Kindly use this mirror through the courtesy of Stephen Henderson," replied the cloaked man, with a grin. He stepped back a ways, eyes intent.

The girl turned her head and favoured him with a slow,

impish smile. "Haven't you ever seen powder used before?" she asked.

"Didn't know angels indulged in cosmetics," Henderson replied. "But then there's a lot I don't know about angels. From now on I shall make them a special study of mine. There's so much I want to find out. So you'll probably find me following you around with a notebook all evening."

"Notebooks for a vampire?"

"Oh, but I'm a very intelligent vampire – not one of those backwoods Transylvanian types. You'll find me charming, I'm sure."

"Yes, you look like the sure type," the girl mocked. "But an angel and a vampire – that's a queer combination."

"We can reform one another," Henderson pointed out. "Besides, I have a suspicion that there's a bit of the devil in you. That dark cloak over your angel costume; dark angel, you know. Instead of heaven you might hail from my home town."

Henderson was flippant, but underneath his banter cyclonic thoughts whirled. He recalled discussions in the past; cynical observations he had made and believed.

Once, Henderson had declared that there was no such thing as love at first sight, save in books or plays where such a dramatic device served to speed up action. He asserted that people learned about romance from books and plays and accordingly adopted a belief in love at first sight when all one could possibly feel was desire.

And now this Sheila – this blonde angel – had to come along and drive out all thoughts of morbidity, all thoughts of drunkenness and foolish gazings into mirrors, from his mind; had to send him madly plunging into dreams of red lips, ethereal blue eyes and slim white arms.

Something of his feeling had swept into his eyes, and as the girl gazed up at him she felt the truth.

"Well," she breathed, "I hope the inspection pleases."

"A miracle of understatement, that. But there was something I wanted to find out particularly about divinity. Do angels dance?"

"Tactful vampire! The next room?"

Arm in arm they entered the parlour. The merrymakers were in full swing. Liquor had already pitched gaiety at its height, but there was no dancing any longer. Boisterous little grouped couples laughed arm in arm about the room. The usual party gagsters were performing their antics in corners. The superficial atmosphere, which Henderson detested, was fully in evidence.

It was reaction which made Henderson draw himself up to full height and sweep the cloak about his shoulders. Reaction brought the scowl to his pale face, caused him to stalk along in brooding silence. Sheila seemed to regard this as a great joke.

"*Pull* a vampire act on them," she giggled, clutching his arm. Henderson accordingly scowled at the couples, sneered horrendously at the women. And his progress was marked by the turning of heads, the abrupt cessation of chatter. He walked through the long room like Red Death incarnate. Whispers trailed in his wake.

"Who is that man?"

"His eyes – "

"Vampire!"

"Hello, Dracula!" It was Marcus Lindstrom and a sullen-looking brunette in Cleopatra costume who lurched towards Henderson. Host Lindstrom could scarcely stand, and his companion in cups was equally at a loss. Henderson liked the man when sober at the club, but his behaviour at parties had always irritated him. Lindstrom was particularly objectionable in his present condition – it made him boorish.

"M'dear, I want you t' meet a very dear friend of mine.

Yessir, it being Halloween and all, I invited Count Dracula here, t'gether with his daughter. Asked his grandmother, but she's busy tonight at a Black Sabbath – along with Aunt Jemima. Ha! Count, meet my little playmate."

The woman leered up at Henderson.

"Oooh Dracula, what big eyes you have! Oooh, what big teeth you have! Oooh – "

"Really, Marcus," Henderson protested. But the host had turned and shouted to the room.

"Folks, meet the real goods – only genuine living vampire in captivity! Dracula Henderson, only existing vampire with false teeth."

In any other circumstance Henderson would have given Lindstrom a quick, efficient punch in the jaw. But Sheila was at his side, it was a public gathering; better to humour the man's clumsy jests. Why not be a vampire?

Smiling quickly at the girl, Henderson drew himself erect, faced the crowd, and frowned. His hands brushed the cloak. Funny, it still felt cold. Looking down he noticed for the first time that it was a little dirty at the edges; muddy or dusty. But the cold silk slid through his fingers as he drew it across his breast with one long hand. The feeling seemed to inspire him. He opened his eyes wide and let them blaze. His mouth opened. A sense of dramatic power filled him. And he looked at Marcus Lindstrom's soft, fat neck with the vein standing in the whiteness. He looked at the neck, saw the crowd watching him, and then the impulse seized him. He turned, eyes on that creasy neck – that wabbling, creasy neck of the fat man.

Hands darted out. Lindstrom squeaked like a frightened rat. He was a plump, sleek white rat, bursting with blood. Vampires liked blood. Blood from the rat, from the neck of the rat, from the vein in the neck of the rat, from the vein in the neck of the squeaking rat.

"Warm blood."

The deep voice was Henderson's own.

The hands were Henderson's own.

The hands that went around Lindstrom's neck as he spoke, the hands that felt the warmth, that searched out the vein. Henderson's face was bending for the neck, and, as Lindstrom struggled, his grip tightened. Lindstrom's face was turning, turning purple. Blood was rushing to his head. That was good. Blood!

Henderson's mouth opened. He felt the air on his teeth. He bent down towards that fat neck, and then –

"Stop! That's plenty!"

The voice, the cooling voice of Sheila. Her fingers on his arm. Henderson looked up, startled. He released Lindstrom, who sagged with open mouth.

The crowd was staring, and their mouths were all shaped in the instinctive O of amazement.

Sheila whispered, "Bravo! Served him right – but you frightened him!"

Henderson struggled a moment to collect himself. Then he smiled and turned.

"Ladies and gentlemen," he said, "I have just given a slight demonstration to prove to you what our host said of me was entirely correct. I *am* a vampire. Now that you have been given fair warning, I am sure you will be in no further danger. If there is a doctor in the house I can, perhaps, arrange for a blood transfusion."

The O's relaxed and laughter came from startled throats. Hysterical laughter, in part then genuine. Henderson had carried it off. Marcus Lindstrom alone still stared with eyes that held utter fear. *He* knew.

And then the moment broke, for one of the gagsters ran into the room from the elevator. He had gone downstairs and borrowed the apron and cap of a newsboy. Now he raced through the crowd with a bundle of papers under his arm.

"Extra! Extra! Read all about it! Big Halloween Horror! Extra!"

Laughing guests purchased papers. A woman approached Sheila, and Henderson watched the girl walk away in a daze.

"See you later," she called, and her glance sent fire through his veins. Still, he could not forget the terrible feeling that came over him when he had seized Lindstrom. Why?

Automatically he accepted a paper from the shouting pseudo-newsboy. "Big Halloween Horror," he had shouted. What was that?

Blurred eyes searched the paper.

Then Henderson reeled back. That headline! It was an *Extra* after all. Henderson scanned the columns with mounting dread.

"Fire in costumer's . . . shortly after 8 p.m. firemen were summoned to the shop of . . . flames beyond control . . . completely demolished . . . damage estimated at . . . peculiarly enough, name of proprietor unknown . . . skeleton found in –"

"No!" gasped Henderson aloud.

He read, reread *that* closely. The skeleton had been found in a box of earth in the cellar beneath the shop. The box was a coffin. There had been two other boxes, empty. The skeleton had been wrapped in a cloak, undamaged by the flames –

And in the hastily penned box at the bottom of the column were eye-witness comments, written up under scareheads of heavy black type. Neighbours had feared the place. Hungarian neighbourhood, hints of vampirism, of strangers who entered the shop. One man spoke of a cult believed to have held meetings in the place. Superstition about things sold there – love philtres, outlandish charms and weird disguises.

Weird disguises – vampires – cloaks – *his eyes!*

"This is an authentic cloak."

"I will not be using this much longer. Keep it."

Memories of these words screamed through Henderson's brain. He plunged out of the room and rushed to the panel mirror.

A moment, then he flung one arm before his face to shield his eyes from the image that was not there – the missing reflection. *Vampires have no reflections.*

No wonder he looked strange. No wonder arms and necks invited him. He had wanted Lindstrom. Good God!

The cloak had done that, the dark cloak with the stains. The stains of earth, grave-earth. The wearing of the cloak, the cold cloak, had given him the feelings of a true vampire. It was a garment accursed, a thing that had lain on the body of one undead. The rusty stain along one sleeve was blood.

Blood. It would be nice to see blood. To taste its warmth, its red life, flowing.

No. That was insane. He was drunk, crazy.

"Ah. My pale friend, the vampire."

It was Sheila again. And above all horror rose the beating of Henderson's heart. As he looked at her shining eyes, her warm mouth shaped in red invitation, Henderson felt a wave of warmth. He looked at her white throat rising above her dark, shimmering cloak, and another kind of warmth rose. Love, desire, and a – hunger.

She must have seen it in his eyes, but she did not flinch. Instead, her own gaze burned in return.

Sheila loved him, too!

With an impulsive gesture, Henderson ripped the cloak from about his throat. The icy weight lifted. He was free. Somehow, he hadn't wanted to take the cloak off, but he had to. It was a cursed thing, and in another minute he

151

might have taken the girl in his arms, taken her for a kiss and remained to –

But he dared not think of that.

"Tired of masquerading?" she asked. With a similar gesture she, too, removed her cloak and stood revealed in the glory of her angel robe. Her blonde, statuesque perfection forced a gasp to Henderson's throat.

"Angel," he whispered.

"Devil," she mocked.

And suddenly they were embracing. Henderson had taken her cloak in his arm with his own. They stood with lips seeking rapture until Lindstrom and a group moved noisily into the anteroom.

At the sight of Henderson the fat host recoiled.

"You –" he whispered. "You are –"

"Just leaving," Henderson smiled. Grasping the girl's arm, he drew her towards the empty elevator. The door shut on Lindstrom's pale, fear-filled face.

"Were we leaving?" Sheila whispered, snuggling against his shoulder.

"We were. But not for earth. We do not go down into my realm, but up – into yours."

"The roof garden?"

"Exactly, my angelic one. I want to talk to you against the background of your own heavens, kiss you amidst the clouds, and –"

Her lips found his as the car rose.

"Angel and devil. What a match!"

"I thought so, too," the girl confessed. "Will our children have halos or horns?"

"Both, I'm sure."

They stepped out onto the deserted rooftop. And once again it was Halloween.

Henderson felt it. Downstairs it was Lindstrom and his society friends, in a drunken costume party. Here it was night, silence, gloom. No light, no music, no drinking, no chatter which made one party identical with another; one night like all the rest. This night was individual here.

The sky was not blue, but black. Clouds hung like the grey beards of hovering giants peering at the round orange globe of the moon. A cold wind blew from the sea and filled the air with tiny murmurings from afar.

This was the sky that witches flew through to their Sabbath. This was the moon of wizardry, the sable silence of black prayers and whispered invocations. The clouds hid monstrous Presences shambling in summons from afar. It was Halloween.

It was also quite cold.

"Give me my cloak," Sheila whispered. Automatically, Henderson extended the garment, and the girl's body swirled under the dark splendour of the cloth. Her eyes burned up at Henderson with a call he could not resist. He kissed her, trembling.

"You're cold," the girl said. "Put on your cloak."

Yes, Henderson, he thought to himself. Put on your cloak while you stare at her throat. Then, the next time you kiss her you will want her throat and she will give it in love and you will take it in – hunger.

"Put it on, darling – I insist," the girl whispered. Her eyes were impatient, burning with an eagerness to match his own.

Henderson trembled.

Put on the cloak of darkness? The cloak of the grave, the cloak of death, the cloak of the vampire? The evil cloak filled with a cold life of its own that transformed his face, transformed his mind, made his soul instinct with awful hunger?

"Here."

The girl's slim arms were about him, pushing the cloak

153

onto his shoulders. Her fingers brushed his neck, caressingly, as she linked the cloak about his throat.

Henderson shivered.

Then he felt it – through him – that icy coldness turning to a more dreadful heat. He felt himself expand, felt the sneer cross his face. This was Power!

And the girl before him, her eyes taunting, inviting. He saw her ivory neck, her warm slim neck, waiting. It was waiting for him, for his lips.

For his teeth.

No – it couldn't be. He loved her. His love must conquer this madness. Yes, wear the cloak, defy its power, and take her in his arms as a man, not as a fiend. He must. It was the test.

"Sheila." Funny how his voice deepened.

"Yes, dear."

"Sheila, I must tell you this."

Her eyes – so alluring. It would be easy!

"Sheila, please. You read the paper tonight?"

"Yes."

"I . . . I got my cloak there. I can't explain it. You saw how I took Lindstrom. I wanted to go through with it. Do you understand me? I meant to . . . to bite him. Wearing this damnable thing makes me feel like one of those creatures."

Why didn't her stare change? Why didn't she recoil in horror? Such trusting innocence! Didn't she understand? Why didn't she run? Any moment now he might lose control, seize her.

"I love you, Sheila. Believe that. I love you."

"I know." Her eyes gleamed in the moonlight.

"I want to test it. I want to kiss you, wearing this cloak. I want to feel that my love is stronger than this – thing. If I weaken, promise me you'll break away and run, quickly. But don't misunderstand. I must face this feeling and fight it; I want my love for you to be that pure, that secure. Are you afraid?"

"No." Still she stared at him, just as he stared at her throat. If she knew what was in his mind!

"You don't think I'm crazy? I went to this costumer's – he was a horrible little old man – and he gave me the cloak. Actually told me it was a real vampire's. I thought he was joking, but tonight I didn't see myself in the mirror, and I wanted Lindstrom's neck, and I want you. But I must test it."

"You're not crazy. I know. I'm not afraid."

"Then –"

The girl's face mocked. Henderson summoned his strength. He bent forward, his impulses battling. For a moment he stood there under the ghastly orange moon, and his face was twisted in struggle.

And the girl lured.

Her odd, incredibly red lips parted in a silvery, chuckly laugh as her white arms rose from the black cloak she wore to circle his neck gently. "I know – I knew when I looked in the mirror. I knew you had a cloak like mine – got yours where I got mine –"

Queerly, her lips seemed to elude his as he stood frozen for an instant of shock. Then he felt the icy hardness of her sharp little teeth on his throat, a strangely soothing sting, and an engulfing blackness rising over him.

Beetles

WHEN Hartley returned from Egypt, his friends said he had changed. The specific nature of that change was difficult to detect, for none of his acquaintances got more than a casual glimpse of him. He dropped around to the club just once, and then retired to the seclusion of his apartments. His manner was so definitely hostile, so markedly anti-social, that very few of his cronies cared to visit him, and the occasional callers were not received.

It caused considerable talk at the time – gossip rather. Those who remembered Arthur Hartley in the days before his expedition abroad were naturally quite cut up over the drastic metamorphosis in his manner. Hartley had been known as a keen scholar, a singularly erudite fieldworker in his chosen profession of archaeology; but at the same time he had been a peculiarly charming person. He had the worldly flair usually associated with the fictional characters of E. Phillips Oppenheim, and a positively devilish sense of humour which mocked and belittled it. He was the kind of fellow who could order the precise wine at the proper moment, at the same time grinning as though he were as much surprised by it all as his guest of the evening. And most of his friends found this air of culture without ostentation quite engaging. He had carried this urbane sense of the ridiculous over into his work; and while it was known that he was very much interested in archaeology, and a notable figure in the field, he inevitably referred to his studies as "pottering around with old fossils and the old fossils that discovered them."

Consequently, his curious reversal following his trip came as a complete surprise.

All that was definitely known was that he had spent some eight months on a field trip to the Egyptian Sudan. Upon his return he had immediately severed all connections with the institute he had been associated with. Just what had occurred during the expedition was a matter of excited conjecture among his former intimates. But something had definitely happened; it was unmistakable.

The night he spent at the club proved that. He had come in quietly, too quietly. Hartley was one of those persons who usually made an entrance, in the true sense of the word. His tall, graceful figure, attired in the immaculate evening dress so seldom found outside of the pages of melodramatic fiction; his truly leonine head with its Stokowski-like bristle of grey hair; these attributes commanded attention. He could have passed anywhere as a man of the world, or a stage magician awaiting his cue to step onto the platform.

But this evening he entered quietly, unobtrusively. He wore dinner clothes, but his shoulders sagged, and the spring was gone from his walk. His hair was greyer, and it hung pallidly over his tanned forehead. Despite the bronze of Egyptian sun on his features, there was a sickly tinge to his countenance. His eyes peered mistily from amidst unsightly folds. His face seemed to have lost its mould; the mouth hung loosely.

He greeted no one; and took a table alone. Of course cronies came up and chatted, but he did not invite them to join him. And oddly enough, none of them insisted, although normally they would gladly have forced their company upon him and jollied him out of a black mood, which experience had taught them was easily done in his case. Nevertheless, after a few words with Hartley, they all turned away.

They must have felt it even then. Some of them hazarded the opinion that Hartley was still suffering from some form of fever contracted in Egypt, but I do not think they believed this in their hearts. From their shocked descriptions of the man they seemed one and all to sense the peculiar *alien* quality about him. This was an Arthur Hartley they had never known, an aged stranger, with a querulous voice which rose in suspicion when he was questioned about his journey. Stranger he truly was, for he did not even appear to recognize some of the men who greeted him, and when he did it was with an abstracted manner – a clumsy way of wording it, but what else is there to say when an old friend stares blankly into silence upon meeting, and his eyes seem to fasten on far-off terrors that affright him?

That was the strangeness they all grasped in Hartley. He was afraid. Fear bestrode those sagging shoulders. Fear breathed a pallor into that ashy face. Fear grinned into those empty, far-fixed eyes. Fear prompted the suspicion in the voice.

They told me, and that is why I went round to see Arthur Hartley in his rooms. Others had spoken of their efforts, in the week following his appearance at the club, to gain admittance to his apartment. They said he did not answer the bell, and complained that the phone had been disconnected. But that, I reasoned, was fear's work.

I wouldn't let Hartley down. I had been a rather good friend of his – and I may as well confess that I scented a mystery here. The combination proved irresistible. I went up to his flat one afternoon and rang.

No answer. I went into the dim hallway and listened for footsteps, some sign of life from within. No answer. Complete, utter silence. For a moment I thought crazily of suicide, then laughed the dread away. It was absurd – and still, there had been a certain dismayed unanimity in

158

all the reports I had heard of Hartley's mental state. When the stolidest, most hard-headed of the club bores concurred in their estimate of the man's condition, I might well worry. Still, suicide . . .

I rang again, more as a gesture than in expectation of tangible results, and then I turned and descended the stairs. I felt, I recall, a little twinge of inexplicable relief upon leaving the place. The thought of suicide in that gloomy hallway had not been pleasant.

I reached the lower door and opened it, and a familiar figure scurried past me on the landing. I turned. It was Hartley.

For the first time since his return I got a look at the man, and in the hallway shadows he was ghastly. Whatever his condition at the club, a week must have accentuated it tremendously. His head was lowered, and as I greeted him he looked up. His eyes gave me a terrific shock. There was a stranger dwelling in their depths — a haunted stranger. I swear he shook when I addressed him.

He was wearing a tattered topcoat, but it hung loosely over his gauntness. I noticed that he was carrying a large bundle done up in brown paper.

I said something, I don't remember what; at any rate, I was at some pains to conceal my confusion as I greeted him. I was rather insistently cordial, I believe, for I could see that he would just have soon have hurried up the stairs without even speaking to me. The astonishment I felt converted itself into heartiness. Rather reluctantly he invited me up.

We entered the flat, and I noticed that Hartley doublelocked the door behind him. That, to me, characterized his metamorphosis. In the old days, Hartley had always kept open house, in the literal sense of the word. Studies might have kept him late at the institute, but a chance visitor found his door open wide. And now, he double-locked it.

I turned around and surveyed the apartment. Just what I expected to see I cannot say, but certainly my mind was prepared for some sign of radical alteration. There was none. The furniture had not been moved; the pictures hung in their original places; the vast bookcases still stood in the shadows.

Hartley excused himself, entered the bedroom, and presently emerged after discarding his topcoat. Before he sat down he walked over to the mantel and struck a match before a little bronze figurine of Horus. A second later the thick grey spirals of smoke arose in the approved style of exotic fiction, and I smelt the pungent tang of strong incense.

That was the first puzzler. I had unconsciously adopted the attitude of a detective looking for clues – or, perhaps, a psychiatrist ferreting out psychoneurotic tendencies. And the incense was definitely alien to the Arthur Hartley I knew.

"Clears away the smell," he remarked.

I didn't ask "What smell?" Nor did I begin to question him as to his trip, his inexplicable conduct in not answering my correspondence after he left Khartoum, or his avoidance of my company in this week following his return. Instead, I let him talk.

He said nothing at first. His conversation rambled, and behind it all I sensed the abstraction I had been warned about. He spoke of having given up his work, and hinted that he might leave the city shortly and go up to his family home in the country. He had been ill. He was disappointed in Egyptology, and its limitations. He hated darkness. The locust plagues had increased in Kansas.

This rambling was – insane.

I knew it then, and I hugged the thought to me in the

perverse delight which is born of dread. Hartley was mad. "Limitations" of Egyptology. "I hate the dark." "The locusts of Kansas."

But I sat silently when he lighted the great candles about the room; sat silently staring through the incense clouds to where the flaming tapers illuminated his twitching features. And then he broke.

"You are my friend?" he said. There was a question in his voice, a puzzled suspicion in his words that brought sudden pity to me. His derangement was terrible to witness. Still, I nodded gravely.

"You are my friend," he continued. This time the words were a statement. The deep breath which followed betokened resolution on his part.

"Do you know what was in that bundle I brought in?" he asked suddenly.

"No."

"I'll tell you. Insecticide. That's what it was. Insecticide!"

His eyes flamed in triumph which stabbed me.

"I haven't left this house for a week. I dare not spread the plague. They follow me, you know. But today I thought of the way – absurdly simple, too. I went out and bought insecticide. Pounds of it. And liquid spray. Special formula stuff, more deadly than arsenic. Just elementary science, really – but its very prosaicness may defeat the Powers of Evil."

I nodded like a fool, wondering whether I could arrange for him to be taken away that evening. Perhaps my friend, Doctor Sherman, might diagnose . . .

"Now let them come! It's my last chance – the incense doesn't work, and even if I keep the lights burning they creep about the corners. Funny the woodwork holds up; it should be riddled."

What was this?

"But I forgot," said Hartley. "You don't know about it. The plague, I mean. And the curse." He leaned forward and his white hands made octopus-shadows on the wall.

"I used to laugh at it, you know," he said. "Archaeology isn't exactly a pursuit for the superstitious. Too much grovelling in ruins. And putting curses on old pottery and battered statues never seemed important to me. But Egyptology – that's different. It's human bodies, there. Mummified, but still human. And the Egyptians were a great race – they had scientific secrets we haven't yet fathomed, and of course we cannot even begin to approach their concepts in mysticism."

Ah! There was the key! I listened, intently.

"I learned a lot, this last trip. We were after the excavation job in the new tombs up the river. I brushed up on the dynastic periods, and naturally the religious significance entered into it. Oh, I know all the myths – the Bubatis legend, the Isis resurrection theory, the names of Ra, the allegory of Set –

"We found things there, in the tombs – wonderful things. The pottery, the furniture, the bas-reliefs we were able to remove. But the expeditionary reports will be out soon; you can read of it then. We found mummies, too. Cursed mummies."

Now I saw it, or thought I did.

"And I was a fool. I did something I never should have dared to do – for ethical reasons, and for other, more important reasons. Reasons that may cost me my soul."

I had to keep my grip on myself, remember that he was mad, remember that his convincing tones were prompted by the delusions of insanity. Or else, in that dark room I might have easily believed that there was a power which had driven my friend to this haggard brink.

"Yes, I did it, I tell you! I read the Curse of Scarabaeus – sacred beetle, you know – and I did it anyway. I couldn't guess that it was true. I was a sceptic; everyone is sceptical enough until things happen. Those things are like the phenomenon of death; you read about it, realize that it occurs to others, and yet cannot quite conceive of it happening to yourself. And yet it does. The Curse of the Scarabaeus was like that."

Thoughts of the Sacred Beetle of Egypt crossed my mind. And I remembered, also, the seven plagues. And I knew what he would say . . .

"We came back. On the ship I noticed them. They crawled out of the corners every night. When I turned the light on they went away, but they always returned when I tried to sleep. I burned incense to keep them off, and then I moved into a new cabin. But they followed me.

"I did not dare tell anyone. Most of the chaps would have laughed, and the Egyptologists in the party wouldn't have helped much. Besides, I couldn't confess my crime. So I went on alone."

His voice was a dry whisper.

"It was pure hell. One night on the boat I saw the black things crawling in my food. After that I ate in the cabin, alone. I dared not see anyone now, for fear they might notice how the things followed me. They did follow me, you know – if I walked in shadow on the deck they crept along behind. Only the sun kept them back, or a pure flame. I nearly went mad trying to account logically for their presence; trying to imagine how they got on the boat. But all the time I knew in my heart what the truth was. They were a sending – the Curse!

"When I reached port I went up and resigned. When my guilt was discovered there would have been a scandal, anyway, so I resigned. I couldn't hope to continue work with those things crawling all over, wherever I went. I was afraid to look anyone up. Naturally, I tried. That one night at the club was ghastly, though – I could see them marching across the carpet and crawling up the sides of my chair, and it took all there was in me to keep me from screaming and dashing out.

"Since then I've stayed here, alone. Before I decide on any course for the future, I must fight the Curse and win. Nothing else will help."

I started to interject a phrase, but he brushed it aside and continued desperately.

"No, I couldn't go away. They followed me across the ocean; they haunt me in the streets. I could be locked up and they would still come. They come every night and crawl up the sides of my bed and try to get at my face and I must sleep soon or I'll go mad, they crawl over my face at night, they crawl – "

It was horrible to see the words ooze out between his set teeth, for he was fighting madly to control himself.

"Perhaps the insecticide will kill them. It was the first thing I should have thought of, but of course panic confused me. Yes, I put my trust in the insecticide. Grotesque, isn't it? Fighting an ancient curse with insect powder?"

I spoke at last. "They're beetles, aren't they?"

He nodded. "Scarabaeus beetles. You know the curse. The mummies under the protection of the Scarab cannot be violated."

I knew the curse. It was one of the oldest known to history. Like all legends, it had had a persistent life. Perhaps I could reason.

"But why should it affect you?" I asked. Yes, I would reason with Hartley. Egyptian fever had deranged him, and the colourful curse story had gripped his mind. If I spoke logically, I might get him to understand his hallucination. "Why should it affect you?" I repeated.

He was silent for a moment before he spoke, and then his words seemed to be wrung out of him.

"I stole a mummy," he said. "I stole the mummy of a temple virgin. I must have been crazy to do it; something happens to you under that sun. There was gold in the case, and jewels, and ornaments. And there was the Curse, written. I got them – both."

I stared at him, and knew that in this he spoke the truth.

"That's why I cannot keep up my work. I stole the mummy, and I am cursed. I didn't believe, but the crawling things came just as the inscription said.

"At first I thought that was the meaning of the Curse, that wherever I went the beetles would go, too, that they would haunt me and keep me from men forever. But lately I am beginning to think differently. I think the beetles will act as messengers of vengeance. I think they mean to kill me."

This was pure raving.

"I haven't dared open the mummy-case since. I'm afraid to read the inscription again. I have it here in the house, but I've locked it up and I won't show you. I want to burn it – but I must keep it on hand. In a way, it's the only proof of my sanity. And if the things kill me – "

"Snap out of it," I commanded. Then I started. I don't know the exact words I used, but I said reassuring, hearty, wholesome things. And when I finished he smiled the martyred smile of the obsessed.

"Delusions? They're real. But where do they come from? I can't find any cracks in the woodwork. The walls are sound. And yet every night the beetles come and crawl up the bed and try to get at my face. They don't bite, they merely crawl. There are thousands of them – black thousands of silent crawling things, inches long. I brush them away, but when I fall asleep they come back; they're clever, and I can't pretend. I've never caught one; they're too fast-moving. They seem to understand me – or the Power that sends them understands.

"They crawl up from Hell night after night, and I can't last much longer. Some evening, I'll fall completely asleep and they will creep over my face, and then – "

He leaped to his feet and screamed.

"The corner – in the corner now – out of the walls –"

The black shadows were moving, marching.

I saw a blur, fancied I could detect rustling forms advancing, creeping, spreading before the light.

Hartley sobbed.

I turned on the electric light. There was, of course, nothing there. I didn't say a word, but left abruptly. Hartley continued to sit huddled in his chair, his head in his hands.

I went straight to my friend, Doctor Sherman.

2

He diagnosed it as I thought he would, phobia, accompanied by hallucinations. Hartley's feeling of guilt over stealing the mummy haunted him. The visions of beetles resulted.

All this Sherman studdied with the mumbo-jumbo technicalities of the professional psychiatrist, but it was simple enough. Together we phoned the institute where Harley had worked. They verified the story, in so far as they knew Hartley had stolen a mummy.

After dinner Sherman had an appointment, but he promised to meet me at ten and go with me again to Hartley's apartment. I was quite insistent about this, for I felt that there was no time to lose. Of course, this was a mawkish attitude on my part, but that strange afternoon session had deeply disturbed me.

I spent the early evening in unnerving reflection. Perhaps that was the way all so-called "Egyptian curses" worked. A guilty conscience on the part of a tomb-looter made him project the shadow of imaginary punishment on himself. He had hallucinations of retribution. That might explain the mysterious Tut-ankh-ahmen deaths; it certainly accounted for the suicides.

And that was why I insisted on Sherman seeing Hartley that same night. I feared suicide very much, for if ever a man was on the verge of complete mental collapse, Arthur Hartley surely was.

It was nearly eleven, however, before Sherman and I rang the bell. There was no answer. We stood in the dark hallway as I vainly rapped, then pounded. The silence only served to augment my anxiety. I was truly afraid, or else I never would have dared using my skeleton key.

As it was, I felt the end justified the means. We entered.

The living-room was bare of occupants. Nothing had changed since the afternoon – I could see that quite clearly, for all the lights were on, and the guttering candle-stumps still smouldered.

· Both Sherman and I smelt the reek of the insecticide quite strongly, and the floor was almost evenly coated with thick white insect powder.

We called, of course, before I ventured to enter the bedroom. It was dark, and I thought it was empty until I turned on the lights and saw the figure huddled beneath the bed-clothes. It was Arthur Hartley, and I needed no second glance to see that his white face was twisted in death.

The reek of insecticide was strongest here, and incense burned; and yet there was another pungent smell – a musty odour, vaguely animal-like.

Sherman stood at my side, staring.

"What shall we do?" I asked.

"I'll get the police on the wire downstairs," he said. "Touch nothing."

He dashed out, and I followed him from the room, sickened. I could not bear to approach the body of my friend – that hideous expression on the face affrighted me. Suicide, murder, heart-attack – I didn't even wish to know the manner of his passing. I was heartsick to think that we had been too late.

I turned from the bedroom and then that damnable scent came to my nostrils redoubled, and I knew "Beetles!"

But how could there be beetles? It was all an illusion in poor Hartley's brain. Even his twisted mind had realized that there were no apertures in the walls to admit them; that they could not be seen about the place.

And still the smell rose on the âir – the reek of death, of decay, of ancient corruption that reigned in Egypt. I followed the scent to the second bedroom, forced the door.

On the bed lay the mummy-case. Hartley had said he locked it up in here. The lid was closed, but ajar.

I opened it. The sides bore inscriptions, and one of them may have pertained to the Scarabaeus Curse. I do not know, for I stared only at the ghastly, unshrouded figure that lay within. It was a mummy, and it had been sucked dry. It was all shell. There was a great cavity in the stomach, and as I peered within I could see a few feebly-crawling forms – inch long, black buttons with great writhing feelers. They shrank back in the light, but not before I saw the scarab patterns on the outer crusted backs.

The secret of the Curse was here – the beetles had dwelt within the body of the mummy! They had eaten it out and nested within, and at night they crawled forth. It was true then!

I screamed once when the thought hit me, and dashed back to Hartley's bedroom. I could hear the sound of footsteps ascending the outer stairs; the police were on their way, but I couldn't wait. I raced into the bedroom, dread tugging at my heart.

Had Hartley's story been true, after all? Were the beetles really messengers of a divine vengeance?

I ran into that bedroom where Arthur Hartley lay, stooped over his huddled figure on the bed. My hands fumbled over the body, searching for a wound. I had to know how he had died.

But there was no blood, there was no mark, and there was no weapon beside him. It had been shock or heart attack, after all. I was strangely relieved when I thought of this. I stood up and eased the body back again on the pillows.

I felt almost glad, because during my search my hands had moved over the body while my eyes roved over the room. I was looking for beetles.

Hartley had feared the beetles – the beetles that crawled out of the mummy. They had crawled every night, if his story was to be believed; crawled into his room, up the bed-posts, across the pillows.

Where were they now? They had left the mummy and disappeared, and Hartley was dead. Where were they?

Suddenly I stared again at Hartley. There was something wrong with the body on the bed. When I had lifted the corpse it seemed singularly light for a man of Hartley's build. As I gazed at him now, he seemed empty of more than life. I peered into that ravaged face more closely, and then I shuddered. For the cords on his neck moved convulsively, his chest seemed to rise and fall, his head fell sideways on the pillow. He lived – or something inside him did!

And then as his twisted features moved, I cried aloud, for I knew how Hartley had died, and what had killed him; knew the secret of the Scarab Curse and why the beetles crawled out of the mummy to seek his bed. I knew what they had meant to do – what, tonight, they had done. I cried aloud as I saw Hartley's face move, in hopes that my voice would drown that dreadful rustling sound which filled the room and came *from inside Hartley's body*.

I knew that the Scarab Curse had killed him, and I screamed quite wildly as his mouth gaped slowly open. Just as I fainted, I saw Arthur Hartley's dead lips part, allowing a rustling swarm of *black Scarabaeus beetles* to pour out across the pillow.

The Faceless God

THE thing on the torture-rack began to moan. There was a grating sound as the lever stretched the iron bed still one more space in length. The moaning grew to a piercing shriek of utter agony.

"Ah," said Doctor Carnoti, "we have him at last."

He bent over the tortured man on the iron grille and smiled tenderly into the anguished face. His eyes, tinged with delicate amusement, took in every detail of the body before him – the swollen legs, raw and angry from the embrace of the fiery boot; the back and shoulders, still crimson from the kiss of the lash; the chest crushed by the caress of the Spiked Coffin. With gentle solitude he surveyed the finishing touches applied by the rack itself – the dislocated shoulders and twisted torso; the broken fingers, the dangling tendons in the lower limbs. He turned his attention to the old man's tormented countenance once again. Then he spoke.

"Well, Hassan. I do not think you will prove stubborn any longer in the face of such – ah – eloquent persuasion. Come now; tell me where I can find this idol of which you speak."

The butchered victim began to sob, and the doctor was forced to kneel beside the bed of pain in order to understand his incoherent mumblings. For perhaps twenty minutes the creature groaned on, and then at last fell silent. Doctor Carnoti rose to his feet once more, a satisfied twinkle in his genial eyes. He made a brief motion to one of the blacks operating the rack machinery. The fellow nodded, and went over to the living horror on the instrument.

171

The black drew his sword. It swished upward, then cleaved down once again.

Doctor Carnoti went out of the room, bolted the door behind him, and climbed the steps to the house above. As he raised the barred trap-door he saw that the sun was shining. The doctor began to whistle. He was very pleased.

2

HE had good reason to be. For several years the doctor had been what is vulgarly known as an "adventurer." He had been a smuggler of antiques, an exploiter of labour on the Upper Nile, and had at times sunk so low as to participate in the forbidden "black goods trade" that flourished at certain ports along the Red Sea. He had come out of Egypt many years ago as an attaché on an archaeological expedition, from which he had been summarily dismissed. The reason for his dismissal is not known, but it was rumoured that he had been caught trying to appropriate certain of the expeditionary trophies. After his exposure and subsequent disgrace, he had disappeared for a while. Several years later he had come back to Cairo and set up an establishment in the native quarter. It was here that he fell into the unscrupulous habits of business which had earned for him a dubious reputation and sizeable profit. He seemed well satisfied with both.

At the present time he was a man of perhaps forty-five years of age, short and heavy-set, with a bullet-shaped head that rested on broad, ape-like shoulders. His thick torso and bulging paunch were supported by a pair of spindly legs that contrasted oddly with the upper portions of his beefy body. Despite his Falstaffian appearance he was a hard and ruthless man. His piggish eyes were filled

,with greed; his fleshy mouth was lustful; his own natural smile was one of avarice.

It was his covetous nature that had led him into his present adventure. Ordinarily he was not a credulous man. The usual tales of lost pyramids, buried treasure and stolen mummies did not impress him. He preferred something more substantial: A contraband consignment of rugs; a bit of smuggled opium; something in the line of illicit human merchandise – these were things he could appreciate and understand.

But this case was different. Extraordinary as it sounded, it meant big money. Carnoti was smart enough to know that many of the great discoveries of Egyptology had been prompted by just such wild rumours as the one he had heard. He also knew the difference between improbable truth and spurious invention. This story sounded like the truth.

In brief, it ran as follows. A certain party of nomads, while engaged in a secret journey with a cargo of illegitimately obtained goods, were traversing a special route of their own. They did not feel that the regular caravan lanes were healthful for them to follow. While travelling near a certain spot they had accidentally espied a curious rock or stone in the sands. The thing had evidently been buried, but long years of shifting and swirling among the dunes above it had served to uncover a portion of the object. They had stopped to inspect it at closer range, and thereby made a startling discovery. The thing projecting from the sand was the head of a statue; an ancient Egyptian statue, with the triple crown of a god! Its black body was still submerged, but the head seemed to be in perfect preservation. It was a very peculiar thing, that head, and none of the natives could or would recognize the deity, though the caravan leaders questioned them closely. The whole thing was an unfathomable mystery. A perfectly preserved statue of an unknown god buried all alone in the southern desert, a long way from any oasis, and two hundred miles from the smallest village!

Evidently the caravan men realized something of its uniqueness; for they ordered that two boulders which lay near by be placed on top of the idol as a marker in case they ever returned. The men did as they were ordered, though they were obviously reluctant, and kept muttering prayers beneath their breath. They seemed very much afraid of the buried image, but only reiterated their ignorance when questioned further concerning it.

After the boulders had been placed, the expedition was forced to journey on, for time did not permit them to unearth the curious figure in its entirety, or attempt to carry it with them. When they returned to the north they told their story, and as most tales were in the habit of doing, it came to the ears of Doctor Carnoti. Carnoti thought fast. It was quite evident that the original discoverers of the idol did not attach any great importance to their find. For this reason the doctor might easily return to the spot and unearth the statue without any trouble, once he knew exactly where it was located.

Carnoti felt that it was worth finding. If it had been a treasure yarn, now, he would have scoffed and unhesitatingly put it down as a cock-and-bull story of the usual variety. But an idol – that was different. He could understand why an ignorant band of Arab smugglers might ignore such a discovery. He could also realize that such a discovery might prove more valuable to him than all the treasure in Egypt. It was easy for him to remember the vague clues and wild hints that had prompted the findings of early explorers. They had followed up many blind leads when first they plumbed the pyramids and racked the temple ruins. All of them were tomb-looters at heart, but their ravishings had made them rich and famous. Why not him, then? If the tale were true and this idol not only buried, but totally unknown as a deity; in perfect condition, and in such an out-of-the-way locality – these facts would create a furor when he exhibited his find. He would be famous! Who knew what hitherto untrodden fields he might open up in archaeology? It was well worth chancing.

But he must not arouse any suspicion. He dared not inquire about the place from any of the Arabs who had been there. That would immediately cause talk. No, he must get his directions from a native in the band. Accordingly, two of his servants picked up Hassan, the old camel-driver, and brought him before Carnoti in his house. But Hassan, when questioned, looked very much afraid. He refused to talk. So Carnoti conducted him into his little reception room in the cellar, where he had been wont to entertain certain recalcitrant guests in the past. Here the doctor, whose knowledge of anatomy stood him in good stead, was able to cajole his visitors into speaking.

So Doctor Carnoti emerged from the cellar in a very pleasant frame of mind. He was rubbing his fat hands when he looked at the map to verify his information, and he went out to dinner with a smiling face.

Two days later he was ready to start. He had hired a small number of natives, so as not to excite undue investigation, and given out to his business acquaintances that he was about to embark on a special trip. He engaged a strange dragoman, and made sure that the fellow would keep his mouth shut. There were several camels in the train, and a number of extra donkeys harnessed to a large empty cart. He took food and water for six days, for he intended to return via river-boat. After the arrangements were completed, the party assembled one morning at a certain spot unknown to official eyes, and the expedition began.

175

3

IT was on the morning of the fourth day that they arrived at last. Carnoti saw the stones from his precarious perch atop the leading camel. He swore delightedly, and despite the hovering heat, dismounted and raced over to the spot where the two boulders lay. A moment later he called the company to a hasty halt and issued orders for the immediate erection of the tents, and the usual preparations for encampment. Utterly disregarding the intolerable warmth of the day, he saw to it that the sweating natives did a thorough job; and then, without allowing them a moment's rest, he instructed them to remove the massive rocks from the resting-place. A crew of straining men managed to topple them over at last, and clear away the underlying sand.

In a few moments there was a loud cry from the gang of labourers, as a black and sinister head came into view. It was a triple-crowned blasphemy. Great spiky cones adorned the top of the ebony diadem, and beneath them were hidden intricately executed designs. He bent down and examined them. They were monstrous, both in subject and in execution. He saw the writhing, worm-like shapes of primal monsters, and headless, slimy creatures from the stars. There were bloated beasts in the robes of men, and ancient Egyptian gods in hideous combat with squirming demons from the gulf. Some of the designs were foul and beyond description, and others hinted of unclean terrors that were old when the world was young. But all were evil; and Carnoti, cold and callous though he was, could not gaze at them without feeling a horror that ate at his brain.

As for the natives, they were openly frightened. The

moment that the top of the image came into view, they began to jabber hysterically. They retreated to the side of the excavation and began to argue and mumble, pointing occasionally at the statue, or at the kneeling figure of the doctor. Absorbed in his inspection, Carnoti failed to catch the body of their remarks, or note the air of menace which radiated from the sullen dragoman. Once or twice he heard some vague references to the name "Nyarlathotep," and a few allusions to "The Demon Messenger."

After completing his scrutiny, the doctor rose to his feet and ordered the men to proceed with the excavation. No one moved. Impatiently he repeated his command. The natives stood by, their heads hung, but their faces were stolid. At last the dragoman stepped forward and began to harangue the *effendi*.

He and his men would never have come with their master had they known what they were expected to do. They would not touch the statue of the god, and they warned the doctor to keep his hands off. It was bad business to incur the wrath of the Old God – the Secret One. But perhaps he had not heard of Nyarlathotep. He was the oldest god of all Egypt; of all the world. He was the God of Resurrection, and Resurrection and the Black Messenger of Karneter. There was a legend that one day he would arise and bring the olden dead to life. And his curse was one to be avoided.

Carnoti, listening, began to lose his temper. Angrily he interrupted, ordering the men to stop gawking and resume their work. He backed up this command with two Colt .32 revolvers. He would take all the blame for this desecration, he shouted, and he was not afraid of any damned stone idol in the world.

The natives seemed properly impressed, both by the revolvers and by his fluent profanity. They began to dig again, timidly averting their eyes from the statue's form.

A few hours' work sufficed for the men to uncover the idol. If the crown of its stony head had hinted of horror, the face and body openly proclaimed it. The image was obscene and shockingly malignant. There was an indescribably *alien* quality about it – it was ageless, unchanging, eternal. Not a scratch marred its black and crudely chiselled surface; during all its many-centuried burial there had been no weathering upon the fiendishly carven features. Carnoti saw it now as it must have looked when it was first buried, and the sight was not good to see.

It resembled a miniature sphinx – a life-sized sphinx with the wings of a vulture and the body of a hyena. There were talons and claws, and upon the squatting, bestial body rested a massive, anthropomorphic head, bearing the ominous triple crown whose dread designs had so singularly excited the natives. But the worst and by far the most hideous feature was the lack of a face upon the ghastly thing. It was a faceless god; the winged faceless god of ancient myth – Nyarlathotep, Mighty Messenger, Stalker among the Stars, and Lord of the Desert.

When Carnoti completed his examination at last, he became almost hysterically happy. He grinned triumphantly into that blank and loathsome countenance – grinned into that faceless orifice that yawned as vacantly as the black void beyond the suns. In his enthusiasm he failed to notice the furtive whispers of the natives and the guides, and disregarded their fearsome glances at the unclean eidolon. Had he not done so, he would have been a wiser man; for these men knew, as all Egypt knows, that Nyarlathotep is the Master of Evil.

Not for nothing had his temples been demolished, his statues destroyed, and his priestcraft crucified in the olden days. There were dark and terrible reasons for prohibiting his worship, and omitting his name from the *Book of the Dead*. All references to the Faceless One were long

178

since deleted from the Sacred Manuscripts, and great pains had been taken to ignore some of his godly attributes, or assign them to some milder deity. In Thoth, Set, Bubastis and Sebek we can trace some of the Master's grisly endowments. It was he, in the most archaic of chronicles, who was ruler of the Underworld. It was he who became the patron of sorcery and the black arts. Once he alone had ruled, and men knew him in all lands, under many names. But that time passed. Men turned away from the worship of evil, and reverenced the good. They did not care for the gruesome sacrifice the Dark God demanded, nor the way his priests ruled. At last the cult was suppressed, and by common consent all references to it were for ever banned, and its records destroyed. But Nyarlathotep had come out of the desert, according to the legend, and to the desert he now returned. Idols were set up in hidden places among the sands, and here the thin, fanatical ranks of true believers still leapt and capered in naked worship, where the cries of shrieking victims echoed only to the ears of the night.

So his legend remained and was handed down in the secret ways of the earth. Time passed. In the north the ice-flow receded, and Atlantis fell. New people overran the land, but the desert folk remained. They viewed the building of the pyramids with amused and cynical eyes. Wait, they counselled. When the Day arrived at last, Nyarlathotep again would come out of the desert, and then woe unto Egypt! For the pyramids would shatter into dust, and temples crumble to ruin. Sunken cities of the sea would rise, and there would be famine and pestilence throughout the land. The stars would change in a most peculiar way, so that the Great Ones could come pulsing from the outer gulf. Then the beasts should give tongue, and prophesy in their anthropoglotism that men shall perish. By these signs, and other apocalyptic portents, the world would know that

Nyarlathotep had returned. Soon he himself would be visible – a dark, faceless man in black, walking, staff in hand, across the desert, but leaving no tracks to mark his way, save that of death. For wherever his footsteps turned, men would surely die, until at last none but true believers remained to welcome him in worship with the Mighty Ones from the gulfs.

Such, in its essence, was the fable of Nyarlathotep. It was older than secret Egypt, more hoary than sea-doomed Atlantis, more ancient than time-forgotten Mu. But it has never been forgotten. In the medieval times this story and its prophecy were carried across Europe by returning crusaders. Thus the Mighty Messenger became the Black Man of the witch-covens; the emissary of Asmodeus and darker gods. His name is mentioned cryptically in the *Necronomicon*, for Alhazred heard it whispered in tales of shadowed Irem. The fabulous *Book of Eibon* hints at the myth in veiled and diverse ways, for it was writ in a far-off time when it was not yet deemed safe to speak of things that had walked upon the earth when it was young. Ludvig Prinn, who travelled in Saracenic lands and learned strange sorceries, awesomely implies his knowledge in the infamous *Mysteries of the Worm*.

But his worship, in late years, seems to have died out. There is no mention of it in Sir James Frazer's *Golden Bough*, and most reputable ethnologists and anthropologists are frankly ignorant of the Faceless One's history. But there are idols still intact, and some whisper of certain caverns beneath the Nile, and of burrows below the Ninth Pyramid. The secret signs and symbols of his worship are gone, but there are some undecipherable hieroglyphs in the Government vaults which are very closely concealed. And men know. By word of mouth the tale has come down through the ages, and there are those who still wait for the Day. By common consent there seem to be certain spots in the desert which are carefully avoided by caravans, and several secluded shrines are shunned by those who remember. For Nyarlathotep is the God of the Desert, and his ways are best left unprofaned.

It was this knowledge which prompted the uneasiness of the natives upon the discovery of that peculiar idol in the sand. When they had first noted the head-dress they had been afraid. As for Doctor Carnoti, his face did not matter to them. They were concerned only with themselves, and their course was plainly apparent. They must flee, and flee at once.

Carnoti paid no attention to them. He was busy making plans for the following day. They would place the idol on a wheeled cart and harness the donkeys. Once back to the river it could be put on board the steamer. What a find. He conjured up pleasant visions of the fame and fortune that would be his. Scavenger, was he? Unsavoury adventurer, eh? Charlatan, cheat, impostor, they had called him. How those smug official eyes would pop when they beheld his discovery! Heaven only knew what vistas this thing might open up. There might be other altars, other idols; tombs and temples too, perhaps. He knew vaguely that there was some absurd legend about the worship of this deity, but if he could only get his hands on a few more natives who could give him the information he wanted . . . He smiled, musingly. Funny, those superstitious myths! The boys were afraid of the statue; that was plainly apparent. The dragoman, now, with his stupid quotations. How did it go? "Nyarlathotep is the Black Messenger of Karneter. He comes from the desert, across the burning sands, and stalks his prey throughout the world, which is the land of his domain." Silly! All Egyptian myths were stupid. Statues with animal heads suddenly coming to life; reincarnation of men and gods, foolish kings building pyramids for mummies. Well, a lot of fools believed it; not only the natives, either. He knew some cranks who credited the stories about the Pharaoh's curse, and the magic of the old priests. There were a lot of wild tales about the ancient tombs and the men who died when they invaded them. No wonder his own simple natives believed such trash! But whether they believed it or not, they were going to move his idol, damn them, even if he had to shoot them down to make them obey.

He went into his tent, well satisfied. The boy served him his meal, and Carnoti dined as heartily as was his wont. Then he decided to retire early, in anticipation of his plans for the following morning. The boys could tend the camp, he decided. Accordingly he lay down on his cot and soon fell into contented, peaceful slumber.

4

It must have been several hours later that he awoke. It was very dark, and the night was strangely still. Once he heard the far-away howl of a hunting jackal, but it soon blended into sombre silence. Surprised at his sudden awakening, Carnoti rose and went to the door of the tent, pulling back the flap to gaze into the open. A moment later he cursed in frenzied rage.

The camp was deserted. The fire had died out, the men and camels had disappeared. Foot-prints, already half obliterated by the sands, showed the silent haste in which the natives had departed. The fools had left him there alone.

He was lost. The knowledge sent a sudden stab of fear to his heart. Lost! The men were gone, the food was gone, the camels and donkeys had disappeared. He had neither weapons nor water, and he was all alone. He stood before the door of the tent and gazed, terrified, at the vast and lonely desert. The moon gleamed like a silver skull in an ebony sky. A sudden hot wind ruffled the endless ocean of sand, and sent it skirling in tiny waves at his feet. Then came silence, ceaseless silence. It was like the silence of the tomb; like the eternal silence of the pyramids, where in crumbling sarcophagi the mummies lie, their dead eyes gazing into unchanging and unending darkness. He felt indescribably small and lonely there in the night, and he was conscious of strange and baleful powers that were weaving the threads of his destiny into a final tragic pattern. Nyarlathotep! He *knew*, and was wreaking in immutable vengeance.

But that was nonsense. He must not let himself be troubled by such fantastic rubbish. That was just another form of desert mirage; a common enough delusion under such circumstances. He must not lose his nerve now. He must face the facts calmly. The men had absconded with the supplies and the horses because of some crazy native superstition. That was real enough. As for the superstition itself, he must not let it bother him. Those frantic and morbid fancies of his would vanish quickly enough with the morning sun.

The morning sun! A terrible thought assailed him – the fearsome reality of the desert at midday. To reach an oasis he would be forced to travel day and night before the lack of food and water weakened him so that he could not go on. There would be no escape once he left this tent; no refuge from that pitiless blazing eye whose glaring rays could scorch his brain to madness. To die in the heat of the desert – that was an unthinkable agony. He must get back; his work was not yet completed. There must be a new expedition to recover the idol. He must get back! Besides, Carnoti did not want to die. His fat lips quivered with fear as he thought of the pain, the torture. He had no desire to suffer the anguish of that fellow he had put on the rack. The poor devil had not looked very pleasant there. Ah no, death was not for the doctor. He must hurry. But where?

He gazed around frantically, trying to get his bearings. The desert mocked him with its monotonous, inscrutable horizon. For a moment black despair clutched at his brain, and then came a sudden inspiration. He must go north, of course. And he recalled, now, the chance words let fall by the dragoman that afternoon. The statue of Nyarlathotep faced north! Jubilantly he ransacked the tent for any remains of food or provisions. There were none. Matches and tobacco he carried, and in his kit he found a hunting-knife. He was almost confident when he left the tent. The rest of the journey would now be childishly simple. He would travel all night and make as much time as he could. His pack-blanket would probably shield him from the noonday sun tomorrow, and in the late afternoon he would resume his course after the worst of the heat had abated. By quick marches tomorrow night, he ought to find himself near the Wadi Hassur oasis upon the following morning. All that remained for him to do was to get out to the idol and set his course, since the tracks of his party in the sand were already obscured.

Triumphantly, he strode across the camp-clearing to the excavation where the image stood. And it was there that he received his greatest shock.

The idol had been reinterred! The workmen had not left the statue violated, but had completely filled in the excavation, even taking the precaution of placing the two original stones over the top. Carnoti could not move them single-handed, and when he realized the extent of this calamity, he was filled with an overpowering dismay. He was defeated. Cursing would do no good, and in his heart he could not even hope to pray. Nyarlathotep – Lord of the Desert!

It was with a new and deathly fear that he began his journey, choosing a course at random, and hoping against hope that the sudden clouds would lift so that he could have the guidance of the stars. But the clouds did not lift, and only the moon grinned grimly down at the stumbling figure that struggled through the sand.

Dervish dreams flitted through Carnoti's consciousness as he walked. Try as he might, the legend of the god haunted him with a sense of impending fulfilment. Vainly he tried to force his drugged mind to forget the suspicions that tormented it. He could not. Over and over again he found himself shivering with fear at the thought of a godly wrath pursuing him to his doom. He had violated a sacred spot, and the Old Ones remember ... "his ways are best left unprofaned" ... "God of the Desert ... that empty countenance. Carnoti swore viciously, and lumbered on, a tiny ant amid mountains of undulating sand.

5

Suddenly it was daylight. The sand faded from purple to violet, then suddenly suffused with an orchid glow. But Carnoti did not see it, for he slept. Long before he had planned, his bloated body had given away beneath the gruelling strain, and the coming of the dawn found him utterly weary and exhausted. His tired legs buckled under him and he collapsed upon the sand, barely managing to draw the blanket over him before he slept.

The sun crept across the brazen sky like a fiery ball of lava, pouring its molten rays upon the flaming sands. Carnoti slept on, but his sleep was far from pleasant. The heat brought him queer and disturbing dreams.

In them he used to see the figure of Nyarlathotep pursuing him on a nightmare flight across the desert of fire.

He was running over a burning plain, unable to stop, while searing pain ate into his charred and blackened feet. Behind him strode the Faceless God, urging him onward with a staff of serpents. He ran on and on; but always the gruesome presence kept pace behind him. His feet became numbed by the scorching agony of the sand. Soon he was hobbling on ghastly, crippled stumps, but despite that torture he dared not stop. The Thing behind him crackled in diabolical mirth, his gigantic laughter rising to the blazing sky.

Carnoti was on his knees now, his crippled legs eaten away into ashy stumps that smouldered acridly even as he crawled. Suddenly the desert became a lake of living flame into which he sank, his scorched body consumed by a blast of livid unendurable torment. He felt the sand lick pitilessly at his arms, his waist, his very throat; and still his dying senses were filled with a monstrous dread of the Faceless One behind him – a dread transcending all pain. Even as he sank into that white-hot inferno he was feebly struggling on. The vengeance of the god must never overtake him! The heat was overpowering him now; it was frying his cracked and bleeding lips, transforming his scorched body into one ghastly ember of burning anguish.

He raised his head for the last time before his boiling brain gave way beneath the agony. There stood the Dark One, and even as Carnoti watched he saw the lean taloned hands reach out to touch his fiery face; saw the dreadful triple-crowned head draw near to him, so that he gazed for one grisly moment into that empty countenance. As he looked he seemed to see something in that black pit of horror – something that was staring at him from illimitable gulfs beyond – something with great flaming eyes that bored into his being with a fury greater than the fires that were consuming him. It told him, wordlessly, that his doom was sealed. Then came a burst of white-hot oblivion, and he sank into the seething sands, the blood bubbling in his veins. But the indescribable horror of that glimpse remained, and the last thing he remembered was the sight of that dreadful, empty countenance and the nameless fear behind it. Then he awoke.

For a moment his relief was so great that he did not notice the sting of the midday sun. Then, bathed in perspiration, he staggered to his feet and felt the stabbing rays bite into his back. He tried to shield his eyes and glance above to get his bearings, but the sky was a bowl of fire. Desperately, he dropped the blanket and began to run. The sand was clinging to his feet, slowing his pace and tripping him. It burned his heels. He felt an intolerable thirst. Already the demons of delirium danced madly in his head. He ran, endlessly, and his dream seemed to become a menacing reality? Was it coming true?

His legs *were* scorched, his body *was* seared. He glanced behind. Thank God there was no figure there – yet! Perhaps, if he kept a grip on himself, he might still make it, in spite of the time he had lost. He raced on. Perhaps a passing caravan – but no, it was far out of the caravan route. Tonight the sunset would give him an accurate course. Tonight.

Damn that heat! Sand all around him. Hills of it, mountains. All alike they were, like the crumbled, cyclopean ruins of Titan cities. All were burning, smouldering in the fierce heat.

The day was endless. Time, ever an illusion, lost all meaning. Carnoti's weary body throbbed in bitter anguish, filling each moment with a new and deeper torment. The horizon never changed. No mirage marred the cruel, eternal vista; no shadow gave surcease from the savage glare.

But wait! Was there not a shadow *behind* him? Something dark and shapeless gloated at the back of his brain.

A terrible thought pierced him with sudden realization. Nyarlathotep, God of the Desert! A shadow following him, driving him to destruction. Those legends – the natives warned him, his dreams warned him, even that dying creature on the rack The Mighty Messenger always claims his own . . . a black man with a staff of serpents . . . "He cometh from out the desert, across the burning sands, and stalketh his prey throughout the land of his domain."

Hallucination? Dared he glance back? He turned his fever-addled head. Yes! *It was true, this time.* There *was* something behind him, far away on the slope below; something black and nebulous that seemed to pad on stealthy feet. With a muttered curse, Carnoti began to run. Why had he ever touched that image? If he got out of this he would never return to the accursed spot again. The legends were true. God of the Desert.

He ran on, even though the sun showered bloody kisses on his brow. He was beginning to go blind. There were dazzling constellations whirling before his eyes, and his heart throbbed a shrieking rhythm in his breast. But in his mind there was room for but one thought – escape.

His imagination began playing him strange tricks. He seemed to see statues in the sand – statues like the one he had profaned. Their shapes towered everywhere, writhing giant-like out of the ground and confronting his path with eery menace. Some were in attitudes with wings outspread, others were tentacled and snake-like, but all were faceless and triple-crowned. He felt that he was going mad, until he glanced back and saw that creeping figure now only a half-mile behind. Then he staggered on, screaming incoherently at the grotesque eidolons barring his way. The desert seemed to take on a hideous personality, as though all nature were conspiring to conquer him. The contorted outlines of the sand became imbued with malignant consciousness; the very sun took on an evil like. Carnoti moaned deliriously. Would night never come?

It came at last, but by that time Carnoti did not know it any more. He was a babbling, raving thing, wandering over the shifting sand, and the rising moon looked down on a being that alternately howled and laughed. Presently the figure struggled to its feet and glanced furtively over its shoulder at a shadow that crept close. Then it began to run again, shrieking over and over again the single word, "Nyarlathotep." And all the while the shadow lurked just a little behind.

It seemed to be embodied with a strange and fiendish intelligence, for the shapeless adumbration carefully drove its victim forward in one definite direction, as if purposefully herding it toward an intended goal. The stars now looked upon a sight spawned of delirium – a man, chased across endlessly looming sands by a black shadow. Presently the pursued came to the top of a hill and halted with a scream. The shadow paused in midair and seemed to wait.

Carnoti was looking down at the remains of his own camp, just as he had left it the night before, with the sudden awful realization that he had been driven in a circle back to his starting point. He threw himself forward in one final effort to elude the shadow, and raced straight for the two stones where the statue was buried.

Then occurred that which he had feared. For even as he ran, the ground before him quaked in the throes of a gigantic upheaval. The sand rolled in vast, engulfing waves, away from the base of the two boulders. Through the opening rose the idol, glistening evilly in the moonlight. And the oncoming sand from its base caught Carnoti as he ran toward it, sucking at his legs like a quicksand, and yawing at his waist. At the same instant the peculiar shadow rose and leapt forward. It seemed to merge with the statue in mid-air, a nebulous, animate mist. Then Carnoti, floundering in the grip of the sand, went quite insane with terror.

The formless statue gleamed living in the livid light, and the doomed man stared straight into its unearthly countenance. It was his dream come true, for behind that mask of stone he saw a face with eyes of yellow madness, and in those eyes he read death. The black figure spread its wings against the hills, and sank into the sand with a thunderous crash.

Thereafter nothing remained above the earth save a living head that twisted on the ground and struggled futilely to free its imprisoned body from the iron embrace of the encircling sand. Its imprecations turned to frantic cries for mercy, then sank to a sob in which echoed the single word, "Nyarlathotep."

When morning came Carnoti was still alive, and the sun baked his brain into a hell of crimson agony. But not for long. The vultures winged across the desert plain and descended upon him, almost as if supernaturally summoned.

Somewhere, buried in the sands below, an ancient idol lay, and upon its featureless countenance there was the faintest hint of a monstrous hidden smile. For even as Carnoti the unbeliever died, his mangled lips paid whispered homage to Nyarlathotep, Lord of the Desert.

THE END

Occult and the Unusual in Tandem editions

Horror in Tandem editions

Name...

Address ....

Titles required................................

....

....

....

....

....

....

....

The publishers hope that you enjoyed this book and invite you to write for the full list of Tandem titles which is available free of charge.

If you find any difficulty in obtaining these books from your usual retailer we shall be pleased to supply the titles of your choice — packing and postage 5p — upon receipt of your remittance.

WRITE NOW TO:
      Universal-Tandem Publishing Co. Ltd.,
      14 Gloucester Road,
      London SW7